# The Lemon Table

JULIAN BARNES has published eight other novels, *Metroland*, *Before She Met Me*, *Staring at the Sun*, *Flaubert's Parrot*, *A History of the World in 10½ Chapters*, *Talking It Over*, *The Porcupine*, *England, England*, and *Love, etc*; a book of short stories, *Cross Channel*; and also two collections of essays, *Letters from London* and *Something to Declare*. His work has been translated into more than thirty languages. In France he is the only writer to have won both the Prix Médicis (for *Flaubert's Parrot*) and the Prix Fémina (for *Talking It Over*). In 1993 he was awarded the Shakespeare Prize by the FVS Foundation of Hamburg. He lives in London.

## By the same author

# Julian Barnes

# The Lemon Table

PICADOR

First published 2004 by Jonathan Cape

This edition published 2005 by Picador
an imprint of Pan Macmillan Ltd
Pan Macmillan, 20 New Wharf Road, London N1 9RR
Basingstoke and Oxford
Associated companies throughout the world
www.panmacmillan.com

ISBN 0 330 42692 3

1 3 5 7 9 8 6 4 2

A CIP catalogue record for this book is available from
the British Library.

Printed and bound in Great Britain by
Mackays of Chatham plc, Chatham, Kent

*to Pat*

# Contents

# A Short History
# of Hairdressing

# 1

That first time, after they moved, his mother had come with him. Presumably to examine the barber. As if the phrase 'short back and sides, with a little bit off the top' might mean something different in this new suburb. He'd doubted it. Everything else seemed the same: the torture chair, the surgical smells, the strop and the folded razor – folded not in safety but in threat. Most of all, the torturer-in-chief was the same, a loony with big hands who pushed your head down till your windpipe nearly snapped, who prodded your ear with a bamboo finger. 'General inspection, madam?' he said greasily when he'd finished. His mother had shaken off the effects of her magazine and stood up. 'Very nice,' she said vaguely, leaning over him, smelling of stuff. 'I'll send him by himself next time.' Outside, she had rubbed his cheek, looked at him with idle eyes, and murmured, 'You poor shorn lamb.'

Now he was on his own. As he walked past the estate agent's, the sports shop and the half-timbered bank, he prac-tised saying, 'Short back and sides with a little bit off the top.' He said it urgently, without the commas; you had to get the words just right, like a prayer. There was one and threepence in his pocket; he stuffed his handkerchief in tighter to keep the coins safe. He didn't like not being allowed to be afraid. It was simpler at the dentist's: your mother always came with you, the dentist always hurt you, but afterwards he gave you a boiled sweet for being a good boy, and then back in the waiting room you pretended in front of the other patients that you were made of stern stuff. Your parents were proud of you. 'Been in the wars, old chap?' his father would ask. Pain let you into the world of grown-up phrases. The dentist would say, 'Tell your father you're fit for overseas. He'll understand.' So he'd go home and Dad would say, 'Been in the wars, old chap?' and he'd answer, 'Mr Gordon says I'm fit for overseas.'

He felt almost important going in, with the adult spring of the door against his hand. But the barber merely nodded, pointed with his comb to the line of high-backed chairs, and resumed his standing crouch over a white-haired geezer. Gregory sat down. His chair creaked. Already he wanted to pee. There was a bin of magazines next to him, which he didn't dare explore. He gazed at the hamster nests of hair on the floor.

When his turn came, the barber slipped a thick rubber cushion on to the seat. The gesture looked insulting: he'd been in long trousers now for ten and a half months. But that was typical: you were never sure of the rules, never sure if they tortured everyone the same way, or if it was just you. Like now: the barber was trying to strangle him with the sheet, pulling it tight round his neck, then shoving a cloth down inside his collar. 'And what can we do for you today, young man?' The tone implied that such an ignominious and deceitful woodlouse as he obviously was might have strayed into the premises for any number of different reasons.

After a pause, Gregory said, 'I'd like a haircut, please.'

'Well, I'd say you'd come to the right place, wouldn't you?' The barber tapped him on the crown with his comb; not painfully, but not lightly either.

'Short-back-and-sides-with-a-little-bit-off-the-top-please.'

'Now we're motoring,' said the barber.

They would only do boys at certain times of the week.

4

There was a notice saying No Boys On Saturday Mornings. Saturday afternoons they were closed anyway, so it might just as well read No Boys On Saturdays. Boys had to go when men didn't want to. At least, not men with jobs. He went at times when the other customers were pensioners. There were three barbers, all of middle age, in white coats, dividing their time between the young and the old. They greased up to these throat-clearing old geezers, made mysterious conversation with them, put on a show of being keen on their trade. The old geezers wore coats and scarves even in summer, and gave tips as they left. Gregory would watch the transaction out of the corner of his eye. One man giving another man money, a secret half-handshake with both pretending the exchange wasn't being made.

Boys didn't tip. Perhaps that was why barbers hated boys. They paid less and they didn't tip. They also didn't keep still. Or at least, their mothers told them to keep still, they kept still, but this didn't stop the barber bashing their heads with a palm as solid as the flat of a hatchet and muttering, 'Keep *still*.' There were stories of boys who'd had the tops of their ears sliced off because they hadn't kept still. Razors were called cut-throats. All barbers were loonies.

'Wolf cub, are we?' It took Gregory a while to realize that he was being addressed. Then he didn't know whether to keep his head down or look up in the mirror at the barber. Eventually he kept his head down and said, 'No.'

'Boy scout already?'

'No.'

'Crusader?'

Gregory didn't know what that meant. He started to lift his head, but the barber rapped his crown with the comb. 'Keep *still*, I said.' Gregory was so scared of the loony that he was unable to answer, which the barber took as a negative. 'Very fine organization, the Crusaders. You give it a thought.'

Gregory thought of being chopped up by curved Saracen swords, of being staked out in the desert and eaten alive by ants and vultures. Meanwhile, he submitted to the cold smoothness of the scissors – always cold even when they weren't. Eyes tight shut, he endured the tickly torment of hair falling on his face. He sat there, still not looking, convinced that the barber should have stopped cutting ages ago, except that he was such a loony he would probably carry on cutting and cutting until Gregory was bald. Still to come was the stropping of the razor, which meant that your throat was going to be cut; the dry, scrapy feel of the blade next to your ears and on the back of your neck; the fly-whisk shoved into your eyes and nose to get the hair out.

Those were the bits that made you wince every time. But there was also something creepier about the place. He suspected it was rude. Things you didn't know about, or weren't meant to know about, usually turned out to be rude. Like the barber's pole. That was obviously rude. The previous place just had an old bit of painted wood with colours twirling round it. The one here worked by electricity, and moved in whirly circles all the time. That was ruder, he thought. Then there was the binful of magazines. He was sure some of them were rude. Everything was rude if you wanted it to be. This was the great truth about life which he'd only just discovered. Not that he minded. Gregory liked rude things.

Without moving his head, he looked in the next-door mirror at a pensioner two seats away. He'd been yakking on in the sort of loud voice old geezers always had. Now the barber was bent over him with a small pair of round-headed scissors, cutting hairs out of his eyebrows. Then he did the same with his nostrils; then his ears. Snipping great twigs out of his lugholes. Absolutely disgusting. Finally, the barber started brushing powder into the back of the geezer's neck. What was that for?

Now the torturer-in-chief had the clippers out. That was another bit Gregory didn't like. Sometimes they used hand-clippers, like tin-openers, squeak grind squeak grind round the top of his skull till his brains were opened up. But these were the buzzer-clippers, which were even worse, because you could get electrocuted from them. He'd imagined it hundreds of times. The barber buzzes away, doesn't notice what he's doing, hates you anyway because you're a boy, cuts a wodge off your ear, the blood pours all over the clippers, they get a short-circuit and you're electrocuted on the spot. Must have happened millions of times. And the barber always survived because he wore rubber-soled shoes.

At school they swam naked. Mr Lofthouse wore a pouch-thing so they couldn't see his whanger. The boys took off all their clothes, had a shower for lice or verrucas or something, or being smelly in the case of Wood, then jumped into the pool. You leaped up high and landed with the water hitting your balls. That was rude, so you didn't let the master see you doing it. The water made your balls all tight, which made your willy stick out more, and afterwards they towelled themselves dry and looked at one another without looking, sort of sideways, like in the mirror at the barber's. Everyone in the class was the same age, but some were still bald down there; some, like Gregory, had a sort of bar of hair across the top but nothing on their balls; and some, like Hopkinson and Shapiro, were as hairy as men already, and a darker colour, brownish, like Dad's when he'd peeped round the side of a stand-up. At least he had *some* hair, not like Baldy Bristowe and Hall and Wood. But how did Hopkinson and Shapiro get like that? Everyone else had willies; Hopkinson and Shapiro already had whangers.

He wanted to pee. He couldn't. He mustn't think about

peeing. He could hold out till he got home. The Crusaders fought the Saracens and delivered the Holy Land from the Infidel. Like Infidel Castro, sir? That was one of Wood's jokes. They wore crosses on their surcoats. Chainmail must have been hot in Israel. He must stop thinking that he could win a gold medal in a peeing-high-against-a-wall competition.

'Local?' said the barber suddenly. Gregory looked at him in the mirror for the first proper time. Red face, little moustache, glasses, yellowy hair the colour of a school ruler. *Quis custodiet ipsos custodes*, they'd been taught. So who barbers barbers? You could tell this one was a perve as well as a loony. Everyone knew there were millions of perves out there. The swimming master was a perve. After the lesson, when they were shivering in their towels with their balls all tight and their willies plus two whangers sticking out, Mr Lofthouse would walk the length of the poolside, climb on to the springboard, pause till he had their full attention, with his huge muscles and tattoo and arms out and pouch with strings round his buttocks, then take a deep breath, dive in and glide underwater the length of the pool. Twenty-five yards underwater. Then he'd touch and surface and they'd all applaud – not that they really meant it – but he'd ignore them and practise different strokes. He was a perve. Most of the masters were probably perves. There was one who wore a wedding-ring. That proved he was.

And so was this one. 'Do you live locally?' he was saying again. Gregory wasn't falling for that. He'd be coming round to sign him up for the Scouts or the Crusaders. Then he'd be asking Mum if he could take Gregory camping in the woods – except there'd only be one tent, and he'd tell Gregory stories about bears, and even though they'd done geography and he knew bears died out in Britain at about the time of the Crusades, he'd half-believe it if the perve told him there was a bear.

'Not for long,' Gregory replied. That wasn't too clever, he knew at once. They'd only just moved here. The barber would say sneery things to him when he kept on coming in, for years and years and years. Gregory flicked a glance up at the mirror, but the perve wasn't giving anything away. He was doing an absent-minded last snip. Then he dug into Gregory's collar and shook it to make sure as much hair as possible fell down inside his shirt. 'Think about the Crusaders,' he said, as he started pulling out the sheet. 'It might suit you.'

Gregory saw himself reborn from beneath the shroud, unchanged except that his ears now stuck out more. He started to slide forward on the rubber cushion. The comb snapped against his crown, harder now that he had less hair.

'Not so fast, young fellow-me-lad.' The barber ambled down the length of the narrow shop and came back with an oval mirror like a tray. He dipped it to show the back of Gregory's head. Gregory looked into the first mirror, into the second mirror, and out the other side. That wasn't the back of his head. It didn't look like that. He felt himself blush. He wanted to pee. The perve was showing him the back of someone else's head. Black magic. Gregory stared and stared, his colour getting brighter, staring at the back of someone else's head, all shaved and sculpted, until he realized that the only way to get home was to play the perve's game, so he took a final glance at the alien skull, looked boldly higher up the mirror at the barber's indifferent spectacles, and said, quietly, 'Yes.'

# 2

The hairdresser looked down with polite contempt and ran a speculative comb through Gregory's hair: as if, deep down in the undergrowth, there might be some long-lost parting, like a medieval pilgrim trail. A dismissive flip of the comb made the bulk of his hair flap forward over his eyes and down to his chin. From behind the sudden curtain, he thought, Fuck you, Jim. He was only here because Allie wasn't cutting his hair any more. Well, for the moment, anyway. He thought of her now with passionate memory: him in the bath, her washing his hair, then cutting it while he sat there. He'd pull out the plug and she'd hose the bits of cut hair off him with the shower attachment, flirting with the spray, and when he stood up as often as not she'd suck his cock, there and then, just like that, picking off the last bits of cut hair as she did so. Yeah.

'Any particular . . . place . . . sir?' The guy was feigning defeat in his search for a parting.

'Just take it straight back.' Gregory jerked his head revengefully, so that his hair flew back over the top of his head and back where it belonged. He reached out of the wanky nylon robe-thing and finger-combed his hair back into place, then gave it a fluff. Just like it had been when he walked in.

'Any particular . . . length . . . sir?'

'Three inches below the collar. Take the sides up to the bone, just there.' Gregory tapped the line with his middle fingers.

'And would you be requiring a shave while we're about it?'

Fucking cheek. *This* is what a shave looks like nowadays. Only lawyers and engineers and foresters delved into their little sponge bags every morning and hacked away at the stubble like Calvinists. Gregory turned sideways-on to the mirror and squinted back at himself. 'That's the way she likes it,' he said lightly.

'Married, are we, then?'

Watch it, fucker. Don't mess with me. Don't try that complicity stuff. Unless it's just that you're queer. Not that I've got anything against the condition. I'm pro-choice.

'Or are you saving up for that particular torment?'

Gregory didn't bother to reply.

'Twenty-seven years myself,' said the guy as he made his first snips. 'Has its ups and downs like everything else.'

Gregory grunted in an approximately expressive way, like you did at the dentist's when your mouth was full of hardware and the mechanic insisted on telling you a joke.

'Two kids. Well, one's grown up now. The girl's still at home. She'll be up and away before you can turn round. They all fly the coop in the end.'

Gregory looked in the mirror but the fellow wasn't making eye contact, just head down and snipping away. Maybe he wasn't so bad. Apart from being a bore. And, of course, terminally malformed in his psychology by decades of complicity in the exploitative master-servant nexus.

'But perhaps you're not the marrying kind, sir.'

Now hang *on*. Who's accusing who of being queer? He'd always loathed hairdressers, and this one was no exception. Fucking provincial mister two-point-four children, pay the mortgage, wash the car and put it back in the garage. Nice little allotment down by the railway, pug-faced wife hanging out the washing on one of those metal carousel-things, yeah, yeah, see it all. Probably does a bit of refereeing on Saturday afternoons in some crap league. No, not even a referee, just a *linesman*.

Gregory became aware that the fellow was pausing, as if he expected an answer. He expected an answer? What rights did he have in the matter? OK, let's get this guy sorted out.

'Marriage is the only adventure open to the cowardly.'

'Yes, well, I'm sure you're a cleverer man than me, sir,' replied the hairdresser, in a tone that wasn't obviously deferential. 'What with being at the university.'

Gregory merely grunted again.

'Of course, I'm no judge, but it always seems to me that universities teach the students to despise more things than they have a right to. It's our money they're using, after all. I'm just glad my boy went to the tech. Hasn't done him any harm. He's earning good money now.'

Yeah, yeah, enough to support the next two-point-four children and have a slightly bigger washing machine and a slightly less puggy wife. Well, that was for some. Bloody England. Still, all that was going to be swept away. And this kind of place would be the first to go, stuffy old master-and-servant establishments, all stilted conversation, class-consciousness and tipping. Gregory didn't believe in tipping. He thought it a reinforcement of the deferential society, equally demeaning for tipper and tippee. It degraded social relations. Anyway, he couldn't afford it. And on top of that, he was fucked if he was going to tip a topiarist who accused him of being a shirt-lifter.

These blokes were on the way out. There were places in London designed by architects, where they played the latest hits on a funky sound system, while some groover layered your hair and matched it to your personality. Cost a fortune, apparently, but it was better than *this*. No wonder the place was empty. A cracked Bakelite radio on a high shelf was playing tea-dance stuff. They ought to sell trusses and surgical corsets and support hose. Corner the market in prostheses. Wooden legs, steel hooks for severed hands. Wigs, of course. Why didn't hairdressers sell wigs as well? After all, dentists sold false teeth.

How old was this guy? Gregory looked at him: bony, with haunted eyes, hair cut absurdly short and Brylcreemed flat. Hundred and forty? Gregory tried to work it out. Married twenty-seven years. So: fifty? Forty-five if he got her in the club as soon as he whipped it out. If he'd ever been that adventurous. Hair grey already. Probably his pubic hair was grey as well. Did pubic hair go grey?

The hairdresser finished the hedge-trimming stage, dropped the scissors insultingly into a glass of disinfectant, and took out another, stubbier pair. Snip, snip. Hair, skin, flesh, blood, all so fucking close. Barber-surgeons, that's what they'd been in the old days, when surgery had meant butchery. The red stripe round the traditional barber's pole denoted the strip of cloth wound round your arm when the barber bled you. His shop-sign featured a bowl as well, the bowl which caught the blood. Now they'd dropped all that, and declined into hairdressers. Tenders of allotments, stabbing the earth instead of the extended forearm.

He still couldn't work out why Allie had broken it up. Said he was too possessive, said she couldn't breathe, being with him was like being married. That was a laugh, he'd replied: being with her was like being with someone who was going out with half a dozen other blokes at the same time. That's just what I mean, she said. I love you, he'd said, with sudden desperation. It was the first time he'd said it to anyone, and he knew he'd got it wrong. You were meant to say it when you felt strong, not weak. If you loved me, you'd understand me, she replied. Well, fuck off and breathe, then, he'd said. It was just a row, just a stupid sodding row, that was all. Didn't mean anything. Except it meant they'd broken up.

'Anything on the hair, sir?'

'What?'

'Anything on the hair?'

'No. Never mess with nature.'

The hairdresser sighed, as if messing with nature was what he'd spent the last twenty minutes doing, and that in Gregory's case this all too necessary piece of interference had ended in defeat.

The weekend ahead. New haircut, clean shirt. Two parties. Communal purchase of a pipkin of beer tonight. Get stonking drunk and see what happens: that's my idea of not messing with nature. Ouch. No. Allie. Allie, Allie, Allie. Bind my arm. I hold out my wrists to you, Allie. Wherever you please. Non-medical purposes, but plunge it in. Go on, if you need to. Loose my blood.

'What was that you said just now about marriage?'

'Eh? Oh, the only adventure open to the cowardly.'

'Well, if you don't mind my making a point, sir, marriage has always been very good to me. But I'm sure you're a cleverer man than me, what with being at the university.'

'I was quoting,' said Gregory. 'But I can reassure you that the authority in question was a cleverer man than either of us.'

'So clever he didn't believe in God, I expect?'

Yes, *that* clever, Gregory wanted to say, just *exactly that* clever. But something held him back. He was only brave enough to deny God when among fellow sceptics.

'And, if I may ask, sir, was he the marrying kind?'

Huh. Gregory thought about it. There hadn't been a Madame, had there? Strictly mistresses, he was sure.

'No, I don't think he was the marrying kind, as you put it.'

'Then perhaps, sir, not an expert?'

In the old days, Gregory reflected, barber-shops had been places of ill repute, where idle fellows gathered to exchange the latest news, where lute and viol were played for the entertainment of customers. Now all this was coming back, at least in London. Places full of gossip and music, run by stylists who got their names in the social pages. There were girls in black sweaters who washed your hair first. Wow. Not having to wash your hair before you went out to have it cut. Just saunter in with a hi-sign and settle down with a magazine.

The expert on marriage brought a mirror and showed twin views of his handiwork to Gregory. Pretty neat job, he had to admit, short at the sides, long at the back. Not like some of the blokes in college, who just grew their hair in every direction at the same time, bogbrush beards, Olde Englishe muttonchops, greasy waterfalls down the back, you name it. No, mess with nature just a little bit, that was his real motto. The constant tug between nature and civilization is what keeps us on our toes. Though of course, that did rather beg the question of how you defined nature and how you defined civilization. It wasn't simply the choice between the life of a beast and that of a bourgeois. It was about . . . well, all sorts of things. He had an acute pang for Allie. Bleed me, then bind me up. If he got her back, he'd be less possessive. Except he'd thought of it as just being close, being a couple. She'd liked it at first. Well, she hadn't objected.

He realized that the hairdresser was still holding up the mirror.

'Yes,' he said idly.

The mirror was put down on its face and the wanky nylon robe unwound. A brush swooshed back and forth across his collar. It made him think of a soft-wristed jazz drummer. Swoosh, swoosh. There was lots of life ahead, wasn't there?

The shop was empty, and there was still a glutinous whine from the radio, but even so it was a lowered voice close to his ear which suggested, 'Something for the weekend, sir?'

He wanted to say, Yeah, train ticket to London, appointment with Vidal Sassoon, packet of barbecue sausages, crate of ale, a few herbal cigarettes, music to numb the mind, and a woman who truly likes me. Instead, he lowered his own voice and replied, 'Packet of Fetherlite, please.'

Complicit at last with the hairdresser, he walked out into the bright day calling for the weekend to begin.

## 3

Before setting off, he went into the bathroom, eased the shaving mirror out on its extending arm, flipped it over to the make-up side, and took his nail scissors from his sponge bag. First he trimmed out a few long mattressy eyebrow hairs, then turned slightly so that anything sprouting from his ears would catch the light, and made a snip or two. Faintly depressed, he pushed up his nose and examined the tunnel openings. Nothing of extravagant length; not for the moment. Dampening a corner of his flannel, he scrubbed away behind his ears, bob-sleighed the cartilaginous channels, and gave a final prod into the waxy grottoes. When he looked at his reflection, his ears were bright pink from the pressure, as if he were a frightened boy or a student afraid to kiss.

What was the name for the accretion of stuff that whitened your damp flannel? Ear-crust, he called it. Perhaps doctors had a technical term for it. Were there fungal infections behind the ear, the aural equivalent of athlete's foot? Not very likely: the location was too dry. So maybe ear-crust would do; and maybe everyone had a private name for it, so that no common term was required.

Strange that no one had come up with a new name for the hedge-trimmers and topiarists. First barbers, then hairdressers. Yet when did they last 'dress' hair? 'Stylists'? Fakeposh. 'Crimpers'? Jokey. So was the phrase he used nowadays with Allie. 'Just off to the Barnet Shop,' he'd announce. Barnet. Barnet Fair. Hair.

'Er, three o'clock with Kelly.'

An indigo fingernail stumbled down a row of pencilled capitals. 'Yes. Gregory?'

He nodded. The first time he'd booked over the phone and they'd asked his name he'd replied, 'Cartwright.' There was a pause, so he'd said 'Mr Cartwright,' before realizing what the pause had been about. Now he saw himself upside down in the ledger: GREGGORY.

'Kelly be with you in a minute. Let's get you washed.'

He still, after all these years, couldn't slide easily into the posture. Maybe his spine was going. Eyes half closed, feeling with your nape for the lip of the bowl. Like doing the backstroke and not knowing where the end of the pool was. And then you lay there, with cold porcelain holding your neck and your throat exposed. Upside down, waiting for the guillotine blade.

A fat girl with uninterested hands made the usual conversation with him – 'That too hot?' 'Been on holiday?' 'You want conditioner?' – while half-heartedly attempting with scooped palm to keep the water out of his ears. He had, over the years, settled into a half-amused passivity at the

Barnet Shop. The first time one of these red-faced trainees had asked 'You want conditioner?' he'd answered, 'What do you think?', believing that her superior view of his scalp made her the better judge of his requirements. Stolid logic suggested that something called 'conditioner' could only improve the condition of your hair; on the other hand, why pose the question if there wasn't a valid choice of answer? But requests for advice tended only to confuse, drawing the cautious answer, 'It's up to you.' So he contented himself with saying 'Yes' or 'Not today, thank you', according to whim. Also according to whether or not the girl was good at keeping water out of his ears.

She watchfully half-led him back to the chair, as if drippingness were close to blindness. 'You want a tea, a coffee?'

'Nothing, thanks.'

It wasn't exactly lutes and viols and the assembly of idle fellows exchanging the latest news. But there was stonkingly loud music, a choice of beverage, and a good range of magazines. What had happened to *Reveille* and *Tit-Bits*, which the old geezers used to read, back in the days when he squirmed on the rubber mat? He picked out a copy of *Marie Claire*, the sort of women's mag it was OK for a bloke to be seen reading.

'Hi, Gregory, how are things?'

'Fine. Yourself?'

'Can't complain.'

'Kelly, like the new hair.'

'Yeah. Got bored, you know.'

'Like it. Looks good, falls well. You like it?'

'Not sure.'

'No, it's a winner.'

She smiled. He smiled back. He could do this stuff, customer banter, meant and half-meant. It had only taken him about twenty-five years to get the right tone.

'So what are we doing today?'

He looked up at her in the mirror, a tall girl with a sharp bob he didn't really like; he thought it made her face too angular. But what did he know? He was indifferent to his own hair. Kelly was a restful presence who had quickly understood that he didn't want to be asked about his holidays.

When he didn't reply immediately, she said, 'Shall we splash out and do exactly the same as last time?'

'Good idea.' The same as last time, and next time, and the time beyond that.

The salon had the mixed-ward atmosphere of a jolly outpatients' department where no one had anything serious. Still, he could handle it; social apprehensions were now long gone. The small triumphs of maturity. 'So, Gregory Cartwright, give us an account of your life so far.' 'Well, I've stopped being afraid of religion and barbers.' He'd never joined the Crusaders, whatever they had been; he'd evaded the hot-eyed evangelisers at school and university; now he knew what to do when the doorbell rang on a Sunday morning.

'That'll be God,' he'd say to Allie, 'I'll do it.' And there on the step would be a spruce, polite couple, one of them often black, sometimes with a winning child in tow, and offering an uncontentious opener such as, 'We're just going from house to house asking people if they're worried about the state of the world.' The trick was to avoid both the true Yes and the smug No, because then they had a landing-line across to you. So he would give them a householderish smile and cut to the chase: 'Religion?' And before they in turn could decide whether Yes or No was the correct response to his brutal intuition, he would end the encounter with a brisk, 'Better luck next door.'

Actually, he quite liked having his hair washed; mostly. But the rest of it was mere process. He took only mild pleasure in the bodily contact which was all part of things nowadays. Kelly would lean an unaware hip against his upper arm, or there'd be a brush from another part of her body; and she was never exactly overdressed. Way back when, he'd have thought it was all for him, and be grateful for the draped sheet that covered his lap. Today it didn't stir his mind out of *Marie Claire*.

Kelly was telling him how she'd applied for a job in Miami. On the cruise liners. You went out for five days, a week, ten days, then had shore leave to spend the money you'd earned. She had a girlfriend out there at the moment. Sounded like fun.

'Exciting,' he said. 'When are you off?' He thought: Miami's violent, isn't it? Shootings. Cubans. Vice. Lee Harvey Oswald. Will she be safe? And what about sexual harassment on the cruise ships? She was a nice-looking girl. Sorry, *Marie Claire*, I meant woman. But girl in a way, because she provoked these semi-parental thoughts in someone like him: one who stayed at home, went to work, and had his hair cut. His life, he admitted, had been one long cowardly adventure.

'How old are you?'

'Twenty-*seven*,' said Kelly, as if at the ultimate extremity of youth. Without immediate action her life would be compromised for ever; a couple more weeks would turn her into that old biddy in rollers on the other side of the salon.

'I've a daughter almost your age. Well, she's twenty-five. I mean, we've another one as well. There's two of them.' He didn't seem to be saying it right.

'So how long you been married then?' Kelly asked in quasi-mathematical astonishment.

Gregory looked up at her in the mirror. 'Twenty-eight years.' She gave a larky smile at the idea that anyone could have been married for the enormous length of time that she herself had been alive.

'The elder one's left home, of course,' he said. 'But we've still got Jenny with us.'

'Nice,' said Kelly, but he could see she was bored now. Bored with him, specifically. Just another ageing geezer with thinning hair he'd soon have to comb more carefully. Give me Miami; and soon.

He was afraid of sex. That was the truth. He didn't really know any more what it was for. He enjoyed it when it happened. He imagined, in the years ahead, that there would be gradually less of it, and then, at some point, none at all. But this wasn't what made him afraid. Nor was it anything to do with the daunting specificity with which they wrote about it in magazines. In his younger days they'd had their own daunting specificities. It had all seemed quite clear and bold, back then, when he stood up in the bath and Allie took his cock in her mouth. All that stuff had been self-evident, and imperative in its truth. Now he wondered if he hadn't always got it wrong. He didn't know what sex was for. He didn't think anyone else did either, but that didn't make the situation any better. He wanted to howl. He wanted to howl into the mirror and watch himself howl back.

Kelly's hip was against his bicep, not the edge of her hip either, but the inner curve of it. At least he knew the answer to one of his youthful questions: yes, pubic hair does go grey.

He wasn't worried about the tip. He had a twenty-pound note. Seventeen for the cut, one for the girl who'd washed him and two for Kelly. And just in case they put the price up, he always remembered to bring an extra pound. He was that sort of person, he realized. The man with the back-up pound coin in his pocket.

Now Kelly had finished cutting and stood directly behind him. Her breasts appeared on either side of his head. She took each of his sideburns between thumb and finger, then looked away. This was a trick of hers. Everyone's face is a bit lopsided, she'd told him, so if you judge by eye you can end up making a mistake. She measured by feel, turning away towards the cash-desk and the street. Towards Miami.

Satisfied, she reached for the drier and finger-flicked a soufflé effect which would last until the evening. By now she was on automatic, probably wondering if she had time to pop outside for a ciggie before the next damp head was guided to her. So each time she would forget, and fetch the mirror.

It had been an audacity on his part, some years back. Revolt against the tyranny of the bloody mirror. This side, that side. In forty years and more of going to the barber's, the hairdresser's and the Barnet Shop, he had always assented meekly, whether he recognized the back of his head or not. He would smile and nod, and seeing the nod reproduced in canted glass, would verbalize it into 'Very nice' or 'Much neater' or 'Just the job' or 'Thank you'. If they had clipped a swastika into his nape he would probably have pretended to approve. Then, one day, he thought, No, I don't want to see the back. If the front's OK, the back will be too. That wasn't pretentious, was it? No, it was logical. He was rather proud of his initiative. Of course Kelly always forgot, but that didn't matter. In fact, it was better, since it meant that his timid victory was repeated every time. Now, as she came towards him, her mind in Miami, the mirror dangling, he raised a hand, gave his regular indulgent smile, and said,

'No.'

# THE STORY OF
# MATS ISRAELSON

In front of the church, which contained a carved altar brought from Germany during the Thirty Years War, there stood a row of six horse stalls. Made from white fir cut and seasoned within a gull's cry of the town's crossroads, they were undecorated, even unnumbered. Yet their simplicity and apparent availability were deceptive. In the heads of those who rode to church, and also of those who walked, the stalls were numbered from left to right with the numbers one to six, and were reserved for the six most important men in the neighbourhood. A stranger who imagined he had the right to tie up his horse while enjoying the *Brännvinsbord* at the Centralhotellet, would emerge to find his beast wandering down by the jetty, gazing out at the lake.

Ownership of each individual stall was a matter of private election, either by deed of gift or by last will and testament. But whereas inside the church certain pews were reserved for certain families, from generation to generation, regardless of merit, outside, considerations of civic worth applied. A father might wish to hand on his stall to his eldest son, but if the boy did not show enough seriousness, the gift would reflect upon the father. When Halvar Berggren succumbed to akvavit, frivolity and atheism, and transferred ownership of the third stall to an itinerant knife-grinder, it was on Berggren, not the knife-grinder, that disapproval fell, and a more suitable appointment was made in exchange for a few riksdaler.

There was no surprise when Anders Bodén was awarded the fourth stall. The general manager of the sawmill was noted for his industry, lack of frivolity, and devotion to his family. If he was not unduly devout, he was charitable. One autumn, when the shooting had been good, he had filled one of the sawpits with scrap timber, lain a metal grid across the top, and cooked a deer whose meat he distributed among his workmen. Though not born in the town, he took it upon himself to show others its sights; visitors would find themselves at his insistence climbing the *klockstapel* beside the church. Leaning one arm against the bell-block, Anders would point out the brickworks; beyond it, the deaf-and-dumb asylum; and just out of sight the statue marking the spot where Gustavus Vasa addressed the Dalecarlians in 1520. A hefty, bearded and enthusiastic man, he would even suggest a pilgrimage to the Hökberg, to view the stone recently placed there in memory of the jurist Johannes Stiernbock. In the distance, a steamboat tracked across the lake; below, complacent in its stall, his horse waited.

Gossip said that Anders Bodén spent so long with visitors to the town because this delayed his return home; gossip repeated that the first time he had asked Gertrud to marry him, she had laughed in his beard, and only began to see his virtues after her own disappointment in love with the Markelius boy; gossip speculated that when Gertrud's father had come to Anders and suggested he renew his wooing, negotiations had not been simple. The sawmill manager had previously been made to feel impertinent in approaching a woman as talented and artistic as Gertrud – who, after all, had once played piano duets with Sjögren. But the marriage had prospered as far as gossip could tell, even if she was known to call him a bore on public occasions. There were two children, and the specialist who delivered the second advised Mrs Bodén against further pregnancy.

When the pharmacist Axel Lindwall and his wife Barbro came to town, Anders Bodén took them up the *klockstapel* and offered to walk them to the Hökberg. On his return home, Gertrud asked why he was not wearing the club-button of the Swedish Tourists' Union.

'Because I am not a member.'

'They ought to make you an honorary one,' she replied.

Anders had learnt to deal with his wife's sarcasm by means of pedantry, by answering her questions as if they meant no more than the words they contained. This tended to annoy her further, but for him it was a necessary protection.

'They seem an agreeable couple,' he said, matter-of-factly.

'You like everybody.'

'No, my love, I do not think that is true.' He meant, for instance, that at the present moment he did not like her.

'You are more discriminating about logs than about members of the human race.'

'Logs, my love, are very different from one another.'

The arrival of the Lindwalls in the town caused no special interest. Those who sought Axel Lindwall's professional advice found all they could hope for in a pharmacist: someone slow and serious, who flatteringly regarded all complaints as life-threatening, while at the same time judging them curable. He was a short, flaxen-haired man; gossip wagered he would run to fat. Mrs Lindwall was less remarked upon, being neither menacingly pretty nor contemptibly plain, neither vulgar nor soignée in dress, neither pushy nor reclusive in manner. She was just a new wife, and therefore one who should wait her turn. As incomers, the Lindwalls kept to themselves, which was proper, while regularly attending church, which was also proper. Gossip said that when Axel first handed Barbro into the rowing boat they acquired that summer, she had asked him, anxiously, 'You are sure, Axel, that there are no sharks in the lake?' But gossip, in its honesty, could not be certain that Mrs Lindwall was not making a joke.

Once a fortnight, on a Tuesday, Anders Bodén would take the steamboat up the lake to inspect the seasoning sheds. He was standing at the rail by the first-class cabin when he became aware of a presence beside him.

'Mrs Lindwall.' As he spoke, his wife's words came into his head. 'She's got less chin on her than a squirrel.' Embarrassed, he looked across at the shoreline and said, 'That's the brickworks.'

'Yes.'

A moment later, 'And the deaf-and-dumb asylum.'

'Yes.'

'Of course.' He realized he had already pointed them out to her from the *klockstapel*.

She was wearing a straw boater with a blue ribbon.

Two weeks later she was on the steamer again. She had a sister who lived just beyond Rättvik. He tried to make himself interesting to her. He asked if she and her husband had yet visited the cellar where Gustavus Vasa had been concealed from his Danish pursuers. He explained about the forest, the way its colours and textures changed with the seasons, and how, even from the boat, he could tell the manner in which it was being worked, whereas someone else would merely see a mass of trees. She followed his pointing arm politely; it was perhaps true that in profile her chin was just a little under-hung, and the tip of her nose strangely mobile. He realized that he had never developed a way of talking to women, and that up to now it had never bothered him.

'I'm sorry,' he said. 'My wife maintains that I should be wearing the club-button of the Swedish Tourists' Union.'

'I like a man to tell me what he knows,' replied Mrs Lindwall.

Her words confused him. Were they a criticism of Gertrud, an encouragement to him, or a mere statement of fact?

At supper that evening his wife said, 'What do you talk to Mrs Lindwall about?'

He did not know what to reply, or rather how to reply. But as usual he took refuge in the simplest meaning of the words, and pretended no surprise at the question. 'The forest. I was explaining about the forest.'

'And was she interested? In the forest, I mean.'

'She grew up in the city. She had not seen so many trees until she came to this region.'

'Well,' said Gertrud, 'there are an awful lot of trees in a forest, aren't there, Anders?'

He wanted to say: she was more interested in the forest than you have ever been. He wanted to say: you are unkind about her looks. He wanted to say: who saw me talking to her? He said none of this.

Over the next fortnight, he found himself reflecting that Barbro was a name with a lovely weight to it, and softer-sounding than . . . other names. He thought also that a blue ribbon round a straw hat made his heart cheerful.

On the Tuesday morning, as he was leaving, Gertrud said, 'Give my regards to little Mrs Lindwall.'

He suddenly wanted to say, 'And what if I fall in love with her?' Instead, he replied, 'I shall if I see her.'

On the steamer, he barely managed the normal slow civilities. Before they had cast off, he began telling her what he knew. About timber, how it is grown, transported, hewn. He explained about bastard sawing and quarter sawing. He explained about the three parts of the trunk: pith, heart-wood and sap-wood. In trees which have arrived at maturity, the heart-wood is in the largest proportion, and the sap-wood is firm and elastic. 'A tree is like a man,' he said. 'It takes three score years and ten to arrive at maturity, and is useless after a hundred.'

He told her how once, at Bergsforsen, where an iron bridge spans the rapids, he had watched four hundred men at work, catching the logs as they emerged from the river, and arranging them in the *sorteringsbommar* according to the distinctive marks of their owners. He explained to her, like a man of the world, the different systems of marking. Swedish timber is stencilled in red letters, with inferior wood marked in blue. Norwegian timber is stencilled in blue at both ends with the shipper's initials. Prussian timber is scribed in the sides near the middle. Russian timber is dry-stamped or hammer-marked on the ends. Canadian timber is stencilled in black and white. American timber is marked with red chalk on the sides.

'Have you seen all this?' she asked. He admitted that he had not yet examined North American timber; he had only read about it.

'So each man knows his own log?' she asked.

'Of course. Otherwise a man might steal another's log.' He could not tell if she was laughing at him – indeed, at the whole world of men.

Suddenly there was a flash from the shoreline. She looked away from it, back at him, and in full face the singularities of her profile were brought into harmony: her little chin pushed her lips into prominence, the tip of her nose, her open, grey-blue eyes . . . it was beyond description, beyond even admiration. He felt clever to guess the question in her eyes.

'There is a belvedere. Probably someone with a spyglass.

We are under surveillance.' But he lost confidence as he pronounced the last word. It sounded like something another man might say.

'Why?'

He did not know what to reply. He looked away to the shoreline, where the belvedere flashed again. Embarrassed, he told her the story of Mats Israelson, but he told it in the wrong order, and too quickly, and she did not appear interested. She did not even seem to realize that it was true.

'I'm sorry,' she said, as if aware of his disappointment. 'I have little imagination. I am only interested in what really happens. Legends seem to me . . . silly. We have too many of them in our country. Axel scolds me for having this opinion. He says I am not showing honour to my country. He says that people will take me for a modern woman. But it is not that either. It is that I have little imagination.'

Anders found this sudden speech calming. It was as if she were giving him guidance. Still looking across at the shore, he told her about a visit he had once made to the copper-mine at Falun. He told her only the things that really happened. He told her that it was the greatest copper-mine in the world after those of Lake Superior; that it had been worked since the thirteenth century; that the entrances were close to a vast subsidence in the ground, known as *Stöten*, which had occurred at the end of the seventeenth century; that the deepest shaft was 1300 feet; that nowadays the annual yield was about 400 tons of copper, beside small amounts of silver and gold; that it cost two riksdaler for admission; that gunshots were extra.

'Gunshots are extra?'

'Yes.'

'What are the gunshots for?'

'To awaken the echoes.'

He told her that visitors usually telephoned ahead to the mine from Falun to announce their arrival; that they were given miner's attire and accompanied by a miner; that on the descent the steps were lit by torches; that it cost two riksdaler. He had told her that already. Her eyebrows, he noticed, were strongly marked, and darker than the hair on her head.

She said, 'I would like to visit Falun.'

That evening, he could tell Gertrud was in a temper. Eventually, she said, 'A wife has a right to a husband's discretion when he arranges a rendezvous with his mistress.' Each noun rang like a dead clunk from the *klockstapel*.

He merely looked at her. She continued, 'At least I should be grateful for your naïveté. Other men would at least wait until the steamer was out of sight of the jetty before starting their canoodling.'

'You are deluded,' he said.

'If my father were less of a businessman,' she replied, 'He would shoot you.'

'Then your father should be grateful that the husband of Mrs Alfredsson who runs the *konditori* behind the church in Rättvik is also just such a businessman.' It was too long a sentence, he felt, but it did its work.

That night, Anders Bodén lined up all the insults he had received from his wife and stacked them as neat as any wood-pile. If this is what she is capable of believing, he thought, then this is what is capable of happening. Except that Anders Bodén did not want a mistress, he did not want some woman in a pastry-shop to whom he would give presents and about whom he would boast in rooms where men smoked small cigars together. He thought: of course, now I see, the fact is, I have been in love with her since we first met on the steamboat. I would not have come to it so soon had not

Gertrud helped me there. I never imagined her sarcasm had any use; but this time it did.

For the next two weeks, he did not allow himself to dream. He did not need to dream because everything was now clear and real and decided. He went about his work and in free moments thought about how she had not attended to the story of Mats Israelson. She had assumed it was a legend. He had told it badly, he knew. And so he began practising, like a schoolboy learning a poem. He would tell it her again, and this time she would know, simply from the way he told it, that it was true. It did not take very long. But it was important that he learn to narrate it just as he had narrated the visit to the mine.

In 1719, he began, with some fear that the distant date might bore her, but also convinced that it gave the story authenticity. In 1719, he began, standing on the dock waiting for the return steamer, a body was discovered in the copper-mine of Falun. The body, he continued, watching the shore-line, was that of a young man, Mats Israelson, who had perished in the mines forty-nine years previously. The body, he informed the gulls which were raucously inspecting the boat, was in a state of perfect preservation. The reason for this, he explained in some detail to the belvedere, to the deaf-and-dumb asylum, to the brickworks, was that the fumes of the copper vitriol had inhibited decomposition. They knew that the body was that of Mats Israelson, he murmured to the dockhand on the jetty catching the thrown rope, because it was identified by an aged crone who had once known him. Forty-nine years earlier, he concluded, this time under his breath, in hot sleeplessness as his wife growled gently beside him and a wind flapped the curtain, forty-nine years earlier, when Mats Israelson had disappeared, that old woman, then as young as him, had been his betrothed.

He remembered the way she had been facing him, her hand on the rail so that her wedding ring was not concealed, and had said, simply, 'I would like to visit Falun.' He imagined other women saying to him, 'I long for Stockholm.' Or, 'At nights I dream of Venice.' They would be challenging women in city furs, and they would not be interested in any response except cap-doffing awe. But she had said, 'I would like to visit Falun,' and the simplicity of it had made him unable to answer. He practised saying, with equal simplicity, 'I shall take you there.'

He convinced himself that if he were to tell the story of Mats Israelson correctly, it would make her say once more, 'I would like to visit Falun.' And then he would reply, 'I shall take you there.' And everything would be decided. So he worked at the story until he had it in a form that would please her: simple, hard, true. He would tell it her ten minutes after they cast off, at what he already thought of as their place, by the rail outside the first-class cabin.

He ran through the story one final time as he reached the jetty. It was the first Tuesday in the month of June. You had to be precise about dates. 1719 to begin with. And to end with: the first Tuesday of June in this Year of Our Lord 1898. The sky was bright, the lake was pure, the gulls were discreet, the forest on the hillside behind the town was full of trees that were as straight and honest as a man. She did not come.

Gossip noted that Mrs Lindwall had not kept her rendezvous with Anders Bodén. Gossip suggested there had been a quarrel. Gossip counter-suggested that they had decided on concealment. Gossip wondered if a sawmill manager lucky enough to be married to a woman who owned a piano imported from Germany would really allow his eye to stray to the unexceptional wife of the pharmacist. Gossip replied that Anders Bodén had always been an oaf with sawdust in his hair, and that he was merely seeking out a woman of his own class, as oafs are wont to do. Gossip added that marital relations had not been resumed in the Bodén household since the birth of their second child. Gossip briefly wondered if gossip had invented the whole story, but gossip decided that the worst interpretation of events was usually the safest and, in the end, the truest.

Gossip ceased, or at least diminished, when it was discovered that the reason Mrs Lindwall had not gone to visit her sister was because she was pregnant with the Lindwalls' first child. Gossip thought this a fortuitous rescue of Barbro Lindwall's endangered reputation.

And that was that, thought Anders Bodén. A door opens, and then closes before you have time to walk through it. A man has as much control over his destiny as a log stencilled with red letters which is thrust back into the torrent by men armed with spiked poles. Perhaps he was no more than they said he was: an oaf lucky enough to marry a woman who had once played duets with Sjögren. But if so, and his life, from now on, would never change, then, he realized, neither would he. He would remain frozen, preserved, at this moment – no, at the moment which nearly happened, which could have happened, last week. There was nothing in the world, nothing wife, nor church, nor society could do, to prevent him from deciding that his heart would never move again.

Barbro Lindwall was not convinced of her feelings for Anders Bodén until she recognized that she would now spend the rest of her life with her husband. First there was little Ulf and then, a year later, Karin. Axel doted on the children and so did she. Perhaps that would be enough. Her sister moved to the far north, where cloudberries grew, and sent her pots of yellow jam each season. In the summer, she and Axel went boating on the lake. He put on predictable weight. The children grew. One spring, a labourer from the sawmill swam in front of the steamboat and was run down, the water stained as if he had been taken by a shark. A passenger on the foredeck testified that the man had swum steadily until the last moment. Gossip claimed that the victim's wife had been seen going into the forest with one of his workmates. Gossip added that he was drunk and had taken a bet that he could swim right across the steamer's bows. The coroner decided that he must have been deafened by water in the ears and recorded a verdict of misadventure.

We are just horses in our stalls, Barbro would say to herself. The stalls are unnumbered, but even so we know our places. There is no other life.

But if only he could have read my heart before I did. I do not talk to men like that, listen to them like that, look them in the face like that. Why couldn't he tell?

The first time she had seen him again, each of them part of a couple strolling by the lake after church, she was relieved that she was pregnant because ten minutes later she had a bout of sickness whose cause would otherwise have been obvious. All she could think of, as she vomited into the grass, was that the fingers which held her head belonged to the wrong man.

She never saw Anders Bodén alone; she made sure of that. Once, spotting him board the steamboat ahead of her, she turned back at the jetty. In church she sometimes glimpsed the back of his head, and imagined hearing his voice separately. When she went out, she protected herself with the presence of Axel; at home, she kept the children close. Once, Axel suggested they invite the Bodéns to coffee; she replied that Mrs Bodén would certainly expect Madeira and sponge cake, and even if that was provided would look down her nose at a mere pharmacist and his wife who were both incomers. The suggestion was not repeated.

She did not know how to think about what had happened. There was no one to ask; she thought of similar examples, but they were all disreputable and seemed to have no bearing on her own case. She was unprepared for constant, silent, secret pain. One year, when her sister's cloudberry jam arrived, she looked at a pot, at the glass, the metal lid, the circle of muslin, the handwritten label, the date – the date! – and the occasion for all this, the yellow jam, and she thought: that is what I have done to my heart. And each year, when pots arrived from the north, she thought the same thing.

At first, Anders continued to tell her what he knew, under his breath. Sometimes he was a tourist guide, sometimes a sawmill manager. He could, for instance, have told her about *Defects in Timber*. 'Cup shake' is a natural splitting in the interior of the tree between two of the annular rings. 'Star shake' occurs when there are fissures radiating in several directions. 'Heart shake' is often found in old trees and extends from the pith or heart of the tree towards its circumference.

In subsequent years, when Gertrud scolded, when the akvavit took hold, when polite eyes told him he had indeed become a bore, when the lake froze at its edges and the skating race to Rättvik could be held, when his daughter emerged from church as a married woman and he saw in her eyes more hope than he knew existed, when the long nights began and his heart seemed to close down in hibernation, when his horse stopped suddenly and began to tremble at what it sensed but could not see, when the old steamboat was drydocked one winter and repainted in fresh colours, when friends from Trondheim asked him to show them the copper-mine at Falun and he agreed and then an hour before departure found himself in the bathroom forcing his fingers into his throat to make the vomit come, when the steamer took him past the deaf-and-dumb asylum, when things in the town changed, when things in the town remained the same year after year, when the gulls left their stations by the jetty to scream inside his skull, when his left forefinger had to be amputated at the second joint after he had idly pulled at a stack of timber in one of the seasoning sheds – on these occasions, and many more, he thought of Mats Israelson. And as the years passed, Mats Israelson turned in his mind from a set of clear facts which could be presented as a lover's gift into something vaguer but more powerful. Into a legend, perhaps – a thing she would not have been interested in.

She had said, 'I would like to visit Falun' and all he had needed to reply was, 'I shall take you there.' Perhaps if she had indeed said, flirtatiously, like one of those imagined women, 'I long for Stockholm' or 'At nights I dream of Venice' he would just have thrown his life at her, bought rail tickets the next morning, caused a scandal, and months later come home drunk and pleading. But that was not how he was, because that was not how she was. 'I would like to visit Falun' had been a much more dangerous remark than 'At nights I dream of Venice.'

As the years passed, and her children grew, Barbro Lindwall was sometimes assailed by a terrible apprehension: that her daughter would marry the Bodén boy. That, she thought, would be the worst punishment in the world. But in the event Karin attached herself to Bo Wicander, and could not be teased out of it. Soon, all the Bodén and the Lindwall children were married. Axel became a fat man who wheezed in his pharmacy and secretly feared he might poison someone by mistake. Gertrud Bodén went grey, and a seizure left her one-handed at the piano. Barbro herself first plucked assiduously, then dyed. That she had kept her shape with little assistance from corsetry seemed to her a mockery.

'You have a letter,' Axel said one afternoon. His manner was neutral. He passed it over. The handwriting was unfamiliar, the postmark was Falun.

'Dear Mrs Lindwall, I am in hospital here. There is a matter I would very much like to discuss with you. Would it be possible for you to visit me one Wednesday? Yours truly, Anders Bodén.'

She handed over the letter and watched him read it.

'Well?' he said.

'I should like to visit Falun.'

'Of course.' He meant: of course you would, gossip always called you his mistress; I was never sure, but of course I should have guessed, that is what your sudden cooling and all those years of absent-mindedness were about; of course, of course. But she heard only: of course you must.

'Thank you,' she said. 'I shall take the train. It may be necessary to stay overnight.'

'Of course.'

Anders Bodén lay in bed deciding what to say. At last, after all these years – twenty-three, to be precise – they had finally seen one another's handwriting. This exchange, this first new glimpse of each other, was as intimate as any kiss. Her writing was small, neat, school-formed; it showed no signs of age. He thought, briefly, of all the letters he might have received from her.

At first he imagined that he might simply tell her the story of Mats Israelson again, in the version he had perfected.

Then she would know, and understand. Or would she? Just because the story had been with him every day for more than two decades, this did not mean she would necessarily have any memory of it. So she might judge it a trick, or a game, and things might go wrong.

But it was important not to tell her that he was dying. This would put an unjust burden on her. Worse, sympathy might make her change her reply. He too wanted the truth, not a legend. He told the nursing staff that a dear cousin was coming to visit him, but because of a fragility of the heart must on no account be told of his condition. He asked them to trim his beard and comb his hair. When they had gone, he rubbed a little tooth-powder into his gums, and slid his damaged hand beneath the bedclothes.

At the time of the letter, it had seemed straightforward to her; or, if not straightforward, at least unarguable. For the first time in twenty-three years he had asked something of her; therefore her husband, to whom she had always remained faithful, must grant the request. He had done so, but from that point things began to lose their clarity. What should she wear for the journey? There seemed no clothes for such an occasion, which was neither a holiday nor a funeral. At the station, the booking-clerk had repeated 'Falun', and the stationmaster had eyed her valise. She felt entirely vulnerable – if someone should merely prod her, she would start explaining her life, her purposes, her virtue. 'I am going to meet a man who is dying,' she would have said. 'No doubt he has a last message for me.' This must be the case, mustn't it – that he was dying? Otherwise, it did not make sense. Otherwise, he would have sought contact when the last of their children had left home, when she and Axel had become merely a couple again.

She registered at the Stadshotellet near the marketplace.

Again, she felt the clerk examining her valise, her married status, her motives.

'I am visiting a friend in hospital,' she said, although no question had been asked of her.

In her room, she stared at the hooped iron bedstead, the mattress, the brand-new wardrobe. She had never stayed in a hotel by herself before. This was where women came, she realized – certain women. She felt that gossip could see her now – alone in a room with a bed. It seemed astonishing that Axel had let her come. It seemed astonishing that Anders Bodén had summoned her without any explanation.

Her vulnerability began to disguise itself as irritation. What was she doing here? What was he making her do? She thought of books she had read, the sort Axel disapproved of. In books, scenes in hotel bedrooms were alluded to. In books, couples ran away together – but not when one of them was in hospital. In books, there were heart-warming deathbed nuptials – but not when both parties were still married. So what was to happen? 'There is a matter I would very much like to discuss with you.' *Discuss*? She was a woman in late middle age bringing a pot of cloudberry jam to a man she had known a little, twenty-three years ago. Well, it was up to him to make sense of it all. He was the man, and she had done more than her part just by coming here. She had not remained a respectable married woman all these years merely by chance.

'You have lost weight.'

'They say it suits me,' he replied with a smile. 'They': he obviously meant 'my wife'.

'Where is your wife?'

'She visits on other days.' Which would be apparent to the hospital staff. Oh, his wife visits him on these days, and 'she' visits him when his wife's back is turned.

'I thought you were very ill.'

'No, no,' he replied cheerfully. She seemed very much on edge – yes, it had to be said, a little like a squirrel, with anxious, jumping eyes. Well, he must calm her, soothe her. 'I'm fine. I'll be fine.'

'I thought . . .' she paused. No, things must be clear between them. 'I thought you were dying.'

'I'll last as long as any fir tree on the Hökberg.'

He sat there grinning. His beard had been freshly trimmed, his hair stylishly combed; he wasn't dying after all, and his wife was in another town. She waited.

'That is the roof of the Kristina-Kyrka.'

She turned away, walked to the window, and looked across at the church. When Ulf was little, she always had to turn her back before he would tell her a secret. Perhaps this was what Anders Bodén needed. So she looked at the copper roof blazing in the sun and waited. After all, he was the man.

Her silence, and her turned back, alarmed him. This was not what he had planned. He had not even managed to call her Barbro, casually, as if from long ago. What had she once said? 'I like a man to tell me what he knows.'

'The church was built in the middle of the nineteenth century,' he began. 'I am not sure exactly when.' She did not respond. 'The roof is made from copper extracted from the local mine.' Again no response. 'But I do not know if the roof was constructed at the same time as the church, or if it was a later addition. I intend to find out,' he added, trying to sound purposeful. Still she did not reply. The only voice he heard was Gertrud's, whispering, 'The club-button of the Swedish Tourists' Union.'

Barbro's anger was now with herself as well. Of course she had never known him, never known what he was really like. She had merely indulged a girlish fantasy all these years.

'You are not dying?'

'I'll last as long as any fir tree on the Hökberg.'

'So you are fit enough to come to my room at the Stadshotellet.' She said it as harshly as she could, contemptuous of the whole world of men, with their cigars and mistresses and logs and vain, stupid beards.

'Mrs Lindwall . . .' All clarity of mind deserted him. He wanted to say that he loved her, that he had always loved her, that he thought of her most – no, all of the time. 'I think of you most – no, all of the time,' was what he had prepared to say. And then, 'I have loved you from the moment I met you on the steamboat. You have sustained my life ever since.'

But her irritation made him lose heart. She thought he was just a seducer. So the words he had prepared would seem like those of a seducer. And he did not know her after all. Nor did he know how to talk to women. It enraged him, that there were men out there, smooth-tongued men who knew what best to say. Oh, get it over with, he thought suddenly, catching her irritation. You'll soon be dead anyway, so get it over with.

'I thought,' he said, and his tone was rough, aggressive, like a man bargaining, 'I thought, Mrs Lindwall, that you loved me.'

He saw her shoulders stiffen.

'Ah,' she replied. The vanity of the man. What a false picture she had carried of him all these years, as a person of discretion, tact, of an almost blameworthy inability to put his case. In truth, he was just another man, behaving as men did in books, and she was just another woman for believing otherwise.

Still facing away, she answered him as if he were little Ulf with one of his childish secrets. 'You were mistaken.' Then she turned back to this abject, grinning dandy, this man who evidently knew his way to hotel rooms. 'But thank you' – she wasn't good at sarcasm, and searched briefly for a subject – 'thank you for pointing out to me the deaf-and-dumb asylum.'

She thought about taking back the cloudberry jam, but judged it unseemly. There was still a train she could catch that evening. The idea of staying the night in Falun revolted her.

For a long time Anders Bodén did not think. He watched as the copper roof took on a darker hue. He removed his damaged hand from beneath the bedclothes and used it to make his hair disorderly. He gave the pot of jam to the first nurse who came into the room.

One of the things he had learnt in life, and which he hoped he could rely on, was that a greater pain drives out a lesser one. A strained muscle disappears before toothache, toothache disappears before a crushed finger. He hoped – it was his only hope now – that the pain of cancer, the pain of dying, would drive out the pains of love. It did not seem likely.

When the heart breaks, he thought, it splits like timber, down the full length of the plank. In his first days at the sawmill he had seen Gustaf Olsson take a piece of solid timber, drive in a wedge, and give the wedge a little twist. The timber broke down the grain, from end to end. That was all you needed to know about the heart: where the grain lay. Then with a twist, with a gesture, with a word, you could destroy it.

As night fell and the train began to skirt the darkening lake on which it had all begun, as her shame and self-reproach weakened, she tried to think clearly. It was the only way to keep the pain at bay: to think clearly, to be interested only in what really happens, in what you know to be true. And she knew this: that the man for whom, at any single moment of the last twenty-three years, she would have left husband and children, for whom she would have lost her reputation and her place in society, with whom she would have run away to God knows where, was not, and never would have been, worthy of her love. Axel, whom she respected, who was a good father and breadwinner, was much more worthy of it. And yet she did not love him, not if what she had felt for Anders Bodén was the measure of things. This, then, was the desolation of her life, divided between not loving a man who deserved it, and loving one who did not. What she had thought of as the mainstay of her life, a continuous companion of possibility, as faithful as a shadow or a reflection in water, was no more than that: a shadow, a reflection. Nothing real. Though she prided herself on having little imagination, and though she took no account of legends, she had allowed herself to spend half her life in a frivolous dream. All that could be said for her was that she had kept her virtue. And what sort of claim was that? Had she been tested, she would not have resisted for a moment.

When she thought about it in this way, in clarity and truth, her shame and self-reproach returned, but the more violently. She undid the button of her left sleeve, and unwound from her wrist a length of faded blue ribbon. She let it drop to the floor of the carriage.

Axel Lindwall threw his cigarette into the empty grate when he heard the trap approaching. He took the valise from his wife, helped her down, and paid the driver.

'Axel,' she said, in a tone of bright affection, once they were inside the house, 'why do you always smoke when I am not here?'

He looked at her. He did not know what to do or say.

He did not want to ask her questions in case that made her tell him lies. Or in case that made her tell him the truth. He feared them equally. The silence continued. Well, he thought, we cannot live together in silence for the rest of our lives. So, eventually, he answered, 'Because I like smoking.'

She laughed a little. They were standing in front of the unlit grate; he still held her valise. For all he knew, it contained all the secrets, all the truths and all the lies he did not want to hear.

'I returned sooner than I thought.'

'Yes.'

'I decided not to spend the night in Falun.'

'Yes.'

'The town smells of copper.'

'Yes.'

'But the roof of the Kristina-Kyrka blazes in the setting sun.'

'So I have been told.'

It was painful for him to watch his wife in such a state. It would only be humane to let her tell whatever lies she had prepared. So he allowed himself a question.

'And how is . . . he?'

'Oh, he is very well.' She did not know how absurd this sounded until she had said it. 'That is to say, he is in the hospital. He is very well, but I suspect this cannot be the case.'

'Generally speaking, people who are very well do not go to hospital.'

'No.'

He regretted his sarcasm. A teacher had once told his class that sarcasm was a moral weakness. Why did he remember that now?

'And . . . ?'

She had not realized until now that she would have to

46

account for her visit to Falun; not its incidentals, but its purpose. She had imagined, when she left, that on her return everything would be quite changed, and that it would merely be necessary to explain this change, whatever it might be. As the silence prolonged itself, she panicked.

'He wishes you to have his stall. At church. It is number 4.'

'I know it is number 4. Now go to bed.'

'Axel,' she said, 'I was thinking on the train that we can become old. The sooner the better. I think things must be easier if you are old. Do you think that is possible?'

'Go to bed.'

Alone, he lit another cigarette. Her lie was so preposterous it might even have been true. But it came to the same thing. If it was a lie, then the truth was that she had gone, more openly than ever before, to visit her lover. Her former lover? If it was the truth, Bodén's gift was a sarcastic payment by the jeering lover to the wronged husband. The sort of gift that gossip loved and never forgot.

Tomorrow the rest of his life would start. And it would be changed, quite changed, by the knowledge of how much of his life up till then had not been as he thought. Would he have any memories, any past, that would remain untainted by what had been confirmed tonight? Perhaps she was right, and they should try to be old together, and rely, over time, on the hardening of the heart.

'What was that?' asked the nurse. This one was starting to become incoherent. It was often the case in the final stages.

'The extra . . .'

'Yes?'

'The extra is for gunshots.'

'Gunshots?'

'To awaken the echoes.'

'Yes?'

His voice toiled as he repeated the sentence. 'The extra is for gunshots to awaken the echoes.'

'I'm sorry, Mr Bodén, I don't know what you're talking about.'

'Then I hope you never find out.'

At the funeral of Anders Bodén, his coffin, made from white fir cut and seasoned within a gull's cry of the town's crossroads, was placed in front of the carved altar brought from Germany during the Thirty Years War. The vicar praised the sawmill manager as a tall tree which had fallen beneath God's axe. It was not the first time that the congregation had heard this comparison. Outside the church, stall number 4 stood empty in homage to the dead man. He had made no provision in his will, and his son had moved to Stockholm. After suitable consultation, the stall was awarded to the captain of the steamboat, a man conspicuous for his civic merit.

# THE THINGS YOU KNOW

# 1

'Coffee, ladies?'

They both looked up at the waiter, but he was already advancing the flask towards Merrill's cup. When he'd finished pouring, he moved his eyes, not to Janice, but to Janice's cup. She covered it with her hand. Even after all these years, she didn't understand why Americans wanted coffee immediately the waiter arrived. They drank hot coffee, then cold orange juice, then more coffee. It didn't make sense at all.

'No coffee?' the waiter asked, as if her gesture could have been ambiguous. He wore a green linen apron and his hair was so gelled that you could see every comb-mark.

'I'll have tea. Later.'

'English Breakfast, Orange Pekoe, Earl Grey?'

'English Breakfast. But later.'

The waiter moved off as though offended, and still without making eye contact. Janice wasn't surprised, let alone hurt. They were two elderly ladies and he was probably a homosexual. It seemed to her that American waiters were becoming more and more homosexual, or at least more and more openly so. Perhaps they always had been. It must, after all, be a good way to meet lonely businessmen. Assuming that lonely businessmen were themselves homosexual, which wasn't, she admitted, necessarily the case.

'I like the look of the poached egg,' said Merrill.

'Poached egg sounds nice.' But Janice's agreement didn't mean she'd be ordering it. She thought poached egg was lunch, not breakfast. There were a lot of things on this menu that weren't breakfast either in her book: waffles, home-style pancakes, Arctic halibut. Fish for breakfast? That had never made sense to her. Bill used to like kippers, but she would only let him have them when they were staying at a hotel. They stank the kitchen out, she'd tell him. And they repeated all day. Which was largely, though not entirely, his problem, but still. It had been a matter of some contention between them.

'Bill used to love a kipper,' she said fondly.

Merrill glanced at her, wondering whether she'd missed some logical step in the conversation.

'Of course, you never knew Bill,' said Janice, as if it had been a solecism on Bill's part – one for which she was now apologizing – to have died before he could meet Merrill.

'My dear,' said Merrill, 'with me it's Tom this, Tom that, you have to stop me or I'm off and running.'

They settled down with the menu again, now that the terms on which breakfast was to be conducted had somehow been agreed.

'We went to see *The Thin Red Line*,' said Janice. 'We enjoyed it very much.'

Merrill wondered who 'we' might be. 'We' would have meant 'Bill and I' at one time. Who did it mean now? Or was it just a habit? Perhaps Janice, even after three years of widowhood, couldn't bear to slip back into 'I'.

'I didn't like it,' said Merrill.

'Oh.' Janice gave a sidelong glance to her menu, as if looking for a prompt. 'We thought it was very well filmed.'

'Yes,' said Merrill. 'But I found it, well, boring.'

'We didn't like *Little Voice*,' said Janice, as an offering.

'Oh, I *loved* it.'

'To tell you the truth, we only went for Michael Caine.'

'Oh, I *loved* it.'

'Do you think he's won an Oscar?'

'Michael Caine? For *Little Voice*?'

'No, I mean – generally.'

'Generally? I should think so. After all this time.'

'After all this time, yes. He must be nearly as old as us by now.'

'Do you think so?' In Merrill's opinion, Janice talked far too much about getting old, or at least older. It must be on account of being so European.

'Or if not now, he soon will be,' said Janice. They both thought about this, and then laughed. Not that Merrill agreed, even allowing for the joke. That was the thing about movie stars, they managed not to age at the normal rate. Nothing to do with the surgery either. They somehow remained the age they were when you first saw them. Even when they started playing maturer characters, you didn't really believe it; you still thought of them as young, but acting old – and often not very convincingly.

Merrill was fond of Janice, but always found her a little dowdy. She did insist on greys and pale greens and beiges, and she'd let her hair go streaky-grey which didn't help. It was so natural it looked false. Even that big scarf, pinned across one shoulder in some kind of a gesture, was greeny-grey, for God's sake. And it certainly didn't call for pants, or at least, not pants like those. A pity. She might have been a pretty thing once. Never a beauty, of course. But pretty. Nice eyes. Well, nice enough. Not that she did anything to draw attention to them.

'It's terrible what's happening in the Balkans,' said Janice.

'Yes.' Merrill had long ago stopped reading those pages of the *Sun-Times*.

'Milosevic must be taught a lesson.'

'I don't know what to think.'

'The Serbs never change their spots.'

'I don't know what to think,' repeated Merrill.

'I remember Munich.'

That seemed to clinch the discussion. Janice had been saying 'I remember Munich' a lot lately, though in truth what she meant was that she must, in early childhood, have heard grown-ups referring to Munich as a recent and shameful betrayal. But this wasn't worth explaining; it would only take away from the authority of the statement.

'I might just have the granola and some wholewheat toast.'

'It's what you always have,' Merrill pointed out, though without impatience, more as a matter of indulgent fact.

'Yes, but I like to think I might have something else.' Also, every time she had the granola she had to remember that shaky molar.

'Well, I guess I'll have the poached egg.'

'It's what you always have,' Janice replied. Eggs were binding, kippers repeated, waffles weren't breakfast.

'Will you make the sign for him?'

That was just like Merrill. She always arrived first and chose the seat from which you couldn't catch the waiter's eye without getting a crick in your neck. Which left Janice to flap her hand a few times and try not to get embarrassed when the waiter displayed other priorities. It was as bad as trying to hail a taxi. They just didn't notice you nowadays, she thought.

## 2

They met here, in the breakfast room of the Harborview, among the hurrying businessmen and lounging vacationers, on the first Tuesday of every month. Come rain or shine, they said. Come hell or high water. Actually, it was more, come Janice's hip operation and come Merrill's ill-advised trip to Mexico with her daughter. Apart from that, they'd made it a regular date these last three years.

'I'm ready for my tea now,' said Janice.

'English Breakfast, Orange Pekoe, Earl Grey?'

'English Breakfast.' She said it with a nervous crispness which made the waiter stop checking the table. An indeterminate nod was as near as he came to an apology.

'Coming right up,' he said, as he was already moving off.

'Do you think he's a pansy?' For some reason unknown to her, Janice had deliberately avoided a modern word, though the effect was, if anything, more pointed.

'I couldn't care less,' said Merrill.

'I couldn't care less either,' said Janice. 'Especially not at my age. Anyway, they make very good waiters.' This didn't seem right either, so she added, 'That's what Bill used to say.' Bill hadn't said anything of the kind, as far as she could remember, but his posthumous corroboration was useful when she got flustered.

She looked across at Merrill, who was wearing a burgundy jacket over a purple skirt. On her lapel was a gilt brooch large enough to be a small sculpture. Her hair, cut short, was an improbable bright straw, and seemed not to care that it was unconvincing; instead, it merely said, this is to remind you that I was once a blonde – some sort of blonde, anyway. More an aide-memoire than a hair-colouring, thought Janice. It was a pity about Merrill: she didn't seem to understand that after a certain age women should no longer pretend to be what they had once been. They should submit to time. Neutrality, discretion, dignity were called for. Merrill's refusal must be something to do with being American.

What the two of them had in common, apart from widowhood, were flat suede shoes with special gripper soles. Janice had found them in a mail-order catalogue, and Merrill had surprised her by asking for a pair too. They were very good on wet pavements, as Janice still called them, and it did rain an awful lot up here in the Pacific North-West. People constantly told her it must remind her of England, and she always said Yes, always meaning No.

'I mean, he didn't think they ought to be allowed in the armed forces, but he wasn't prejudiced.'

In response, Merrill stabbed her egg. 'Everyone was a darned sight more discreet about their private business when I was young.'

'Me too,' said Janice hastily. 'I mean, when I was too. Which would have been at about the same time.' Merrill glanced at her, and Janice, reading a reproof, added, 'Though of course in a different part of the world.'

'Tom always said you could tell from the way they walked. Not that it bothers me.' Yet Merrill did seem a little bothered.

'How do they walk?' In asking the question, Janice felt transported back into adolescence, back before marriage.

'Oh, you know,' said Merrill.

Janice watched Merrill eat a mouthful of poached egg. If she was being given a hint, she couldn't imagine what it might be. She hadn't noticed how their waiter walked. 'I don't,' she said, feeling her ignorance as culpable, almost infantile.

'With their hands out,' Merrill wanted to say. Instead, uncharacteristically, she turned her head and shouted, 'Coffee,' surprising both Janice and the waiter. Perhaps she was calling for a demonstration.

When she turned back, she was composed again. 'Tom was in Korea,' she said. 'Oak leaves and clusters.'

'My Bill did his National Service. Well, everyone had to then.'

'It was so cold, if you put your tea on the ground, it turned to a mug of brown ice.'

'He missed Suez. He was in the reserves but they didn't call him up.'

'It was so cold you had to tip your razor out of its case into warm water before you could use it.'

'He quite enjoyed it. He was a good mixer, Bill.'

'It was so cold, if you put your hand on the side of a tank, your skin came away.'

'Probably a better mixer than me, if the truth be known.'

'Even the gas froze solid. The gas.'

'There was a very cold winter back in England. Just after the war. Forty-six, I think, or maybe it was forty-seven.'

Merrill felt suddenly impatient. What did her Tom's suffering have to do with a cold spell in Europe? Really. 'How's your granola?' she asked.

'Hard on the teeth. I've got this molar.' Janice picked a hazelnut out of her bowl and tapped it on the side. 'Looks a bit like a tooth, doesn't it?' She giggled, in a way that further annoyed Merrill. 'What do you think about these implant things?'

'Tom had every tooth in his head when he died.'

'So did Bill.' This was far from true, but it would be letting him down to say anything less.

'They couldn't get a shovel into the ground to bury their dead.'

'Who couldn't?' Under Merrill's stare, Janice worked it out. 'Yes, of course.' She felt herself beginning to panic. 'Well, I suppose it didn't matter in a way.'

'In what way?'

'Oh, nothing.'

'In what way?' Merrill liked to say – to herself and to others – that while she didn't believe in disagreement and unpleasantness, she did believe in telling things straight.

'In . . . well, the . . . people they were waiting to bury . . . if it was that cold . . . you know what I mean.'

Merrill did, but chose to remain implacable. 'A true soldier always buries his dead. You should know that.'

'Yes,' said Janice, remembering *The Thin Red Line* but not liking to mention it. Odd how Merrill chose to comport herself like some high-faluting military widow. Janice knew that Tom had been drafted. Janice knew a thing or two more about him, for that matter. What they said on campus. What she'd seen with her own eyes.

'Of course, I never met your husband, but everyone spoke so highly of him.'

'Tom was wonderful,' said Merrill. 'It was a love match.'

'He was very popular, they all told me.'

'Popular?' Merrill repeated the word as if it were peculiarly inadequate in the circumstances.

'That's what people said.'

'You just have to face the future,' said Merrill. 'Look it full in the face. That's the only way.' Tom had told her this when he was dying.

Better to face the future than the past, thought Janice. Did she really have no idea? Janice remembered a sudden view from a bathroom window, down behind a hedge, a red-faced man unzipping, a woman putting out her hand, the man pushing at her head, the woman refusing, an argument in dumbshow as the party's noise swirled below her, the man putting his hand on the woman's neck, pushing her down, the woman spitting on the man's thing, the man slapping her across the top of the head, all in twenty seconds or so, a cameo of lust and rage, the couple parting, the war hero and love match and famous campus groper zipping himself up again, someone rattling the handle of the bathroom, Janice finding her way downstairs and asking Bill to take her home immediately, Bill commenting on her colour and speculating about that extra glass or two she must have downed when he wasn't looking, Janice snapping at him in the car and then apologizing. Over the years, she had forced herself to forget this scene, pushing it to the back of her mind, almost as if it were about Bill and herself in some way. Then, after Bill had died, and she had met Merrill, there was another reason for trying to forget it.

'People said I would never get over it.' Merrill's manner seemed to Janice monstrously complacent. 'That's the truth. I *shall* never get over it. It was a love match.'

Janice buttered some toast. At least here they didn't deliver your toast already buttered, as they did at some other places. That was another American habit she couldn't get used to. She tried to unscrew the lid of a small pot of honey, but her wrist wasn't strong enough. Then she tried the bramble jelly, with equal lack of success. Merrill seemed not to notice. Janice put a triangle of ungarnished toast into her mouth.

'Bill never looked at another woman in thirty years.' Aggression had risen in Janice like a burp. She preferred to agree with other people in conversation, and she tried to please, but sometimes the pressure of doing this made her say things which surprised her. Not the thing itself, but the fact that she said it. And when Merrill failed to respond, it made her insist.

'Bill never looked at another woman in thirty years.'

'I'm sure you're right, my dear.'

'When he died, I was bereft. Quite bereft. I felt my life had come to an end. Well it has. I try not to feel sorry for myself, I keep myself entertained, no I suppose distracted is more the word, but I know that's my lot, really. I've had my life, and now I've buried it.'

'Tom used to tell me that just seeing me across a room made his heart lift.'

'Bill never forgot a wedding anniversary. Not once in thirty years.'

'Tom used to do this wonderfully romantic thing. We'd go away for the weekend, up into the mountains, and he'd book us into the lodge under a false name. We'd be Tom and Merrill Humphreys, or Tom and Merrill Carpenter, or Tom and Merrill Delivio, and we'd keep it up all weekend, and he'd pay in cash when we left. It made it . . . exciting.'

'Bill pretended to forget one year. No flowers in the morning, and he told me he'd be working late so he'd grab a bite at his desk. I tried not to think about it, but it made me a bit down, and then in the middle of the afternoon I got a call from the car company to check they were to pick me up at seven thirty and take me to The French House. Can you imagine? He'd even thought it out so that they gave me a few hours' warning. And he'd managed to smuggle his best suit into work without me noticing so that he could change into it. *Such* an evening. Ah.'

'I always made an effort before I went to the hospital. I said to myself, Merrill, no matter how darned sorry you feel for yourself, you make sure he sees you looking like something worth living for. I even bought new clothes. He'd say, "Honey, I haven't seen that before, have I?" and give me his smile.'

Janice nodded, imagining the scene differently: the campus groper, on his deathbed, seeing his wife spend money on new clothes to please some successor. As soon as the thought occurred, she felt ashamed of it, and hurried on. 'Bill said that if there was a way to send me a message – afterwards – then he'd find one. He'd get through to me somehow.'

'The doctors told me they'd never seen anyone hang in there so long. They said, the courage of the man. I said, oak leaves and clusters.'

'But I guess even if he was trying to send me a message, I might not be able to recognize the form in which it came. I comfort myself with that. Though the thought of Bill trying to get through and seeing me not understand is unbearable.'

Next she'll be into that reincarnation crap again, thought Merrill. How we all come back as squirrels. Listen, kid, your husband is not only dead, but when he was alive he walked with his hands out, know what I mean? No, she probably wouldn't get it. Your husband was known on campus as that little limey fag in administration – that any clearer? He was a teabag, OK? Not that she would ever actually tell Janice. Far too delicate. She'd just crumble to bits.

It was odd. Knowing this gave Merrill a sense of superiority, but not of power. It made her think, someone's got to look out for her now that little fag husband of hers is gone, and you seem to have volunteered for the job, Merrill. She may irritate the hell out of you from time to time, but Tom would have wanted you to see this one through.

'More coffee, ladies?'

'I'd like some fresh tea, please.'

Janice expected to be offered yet again the choice of English Breakfast, Orange Pekoe or Earl Grey. But the waiter merely took away the miniature, one-cup pot which Americans mysteriously judged sufficient for morning tea.

'How's the hip?' Merrill asked.

'Oh, much easier now. I'm so glad I had it done.'

When the waiter returned, Janice looked at the pot and said sharply, 'I wanted fresh.'

'I'm sorry?'

'I said I wanted fresh. I didn't just ask for more hot water.'

'I'm sorry?'

'This', said Janice, reaching for the yellow label which dangled from the lid of the pot, 'is the same old *teabag*.' She glared at the supercilious young man. She really was cross.

Afterwards, she wondered why he had got all huffy, and why Merrill had suddenly burst into manic laughter, raised her coffee mug, and said, 'Here's to you, my dear.'

Janice raised her own empty cup, and with a dull, unechoing chink, they toasted one another.

## 3

'He's the man to go to for knees. She was driving again in two days.'

'That's quick,' said Merrill.

'I saw Steve the other day.'

'And?'

'Not good.'

'It's heart, isn't it?'

'And he's far too overweight.'

'Never a good idea.'

'Do you think there's a connection between the heart and the heart?'

Merrill gave a smiling shake of the head. She was such a funny little thing, Janice. You never knew which way she would jump. 'I'm not with you there, Janice.'

'Oh, do you think you can get a heart attack from being in love?'

'I don't know.' She gave it some thought. 'I know something else you can get a heart attack from though.' Janice looked puzzled. 'Nelson Rockefeller.'

'What's he got to do with it?'

'That's how he died.'

'What's how he died?'

'They said he was working late on an art book. Well, I never believed that for a minute.' She waited until it was certain Janice had got the point.

'The things you know, Merrill.' And the things I know too.

'Yes, the things I know.'

Janice pushed her breakfast away to make room for her elbows. Half a bowl of granola and a round of toast. Two cups of tea. Liquids went through her so fast nowadays. She looked across at Merrill, at her beaky face and flat, unconvincing hair. She was a friend. And because she was a friend, Janice would protect her from what she knew about that awful husband of hers. It was just as well they had met only as widows; Bill would have loathed Tom.

Yes, she was a friend. And yet . . . Was it more that she was an ally? Like it had been back at the beginning. When you were a child, you thought you had friends, but in fact you only had allies – people on your side who would see you through until you were grown up. Then – in her case – they fell away, and there was being grown up, and Bill, and the children, and the children leaving, and Bill dying. And then? Then you needed allies again, people to see you through until the end. Allies who remembered Munich, who remembered the old films, which were still the best, even if you tried to like the new ones. Allies who helped you understand a tax form and open little pots of jam. Allies who worried just as much about money, even if you suspected that some of them had more of it than they let on.

'Did you hear', Merrill said, 'that Stanhope's deposit has doubled?'

'No, what is it now?'

'A thousand a year. Up from five hundred.'

'Well, it's certainly nice. But the rooms are very small.'

'They're small everywhere.'

'And I shall need two bedrooms. I've got to have two bedrooms.'

'Everyone needs two bedrooms.'

'The rooms at Norton are big. And it's downtown.'

'But the other people are boring, I've heard.'

'Me too.'

'I don't like Wallingford.'

'I don't like Wallingford either.'

'It may have to be Stanhope.'

'If they double the deposit like that you can't be sure they won't double the charges just after you move in.'

'They've got a good scheme where Steve is. They ask you to post a notice saying what you can do to help – like if you can drive someone to hospital or fix up a shelf or know about IRS forms.'

'That's a good idea.'

'As long as it doesn't make you too reliant on others.'

'That's a bad idea.'

'I don't like Wallingford.'

'I don't like Wallingford.'

They looked at one another harmoniously.

'Waiter, would you divide this check?'

'Oh, we can divide it ourselves, Merrill.'

'But I had the egg.'

'Oh, stuff and nonsense.' Janice held out a ten-dollar bill.

'Will that do it?'

'Well, it's twelve if we're sharing.'

Typical Merrill. Typical bloody Merrill. With the money the campus groper left her. A thousand dollars a year just to stay on the waiting list is small change to her. *And* she had the juice as well as the egg. But Janice merely unsnapped her purse, took out two dollar bills, and said, 'Yes, we're sharing.'

# Hygiene

'Right, that's it, me boy.' His kitbag was stowed between the seats, his mackintosh folded beside him. Ticket, wallet, sponge bag, rubber johnnies, tasks list. Tasks bloody list. He held an eyes-front as the train pulled out. None of that soppy stuff for him: the lowered window, the waving hanky, the piping of the eye. Not that you could lower the window any more, you just sat in these cattle trucks with other old fools on cheap tickets and stared out through sealed glass. And not that Pamela'd be there if he did look. She'd be in the car park grinding down the wheel-rims on the concrete kerb as she tried to manoeuvre the Astra closer to the token-slot thingy. She always complained that the men who designed the barriers didn't realize that women had shorter arms than men. He said that was no excuse for playing argy-bargy with the kerb, if you couldn't reach you should just get out, woman. Anyway, that's where she'd be by now, torturing a tyre as her personal part in the battle of the sexes. And she was there already because she didn't want to see him not looking at her from the train. And he was not looking at her from the train because she did insist on adding to his tasks bloody list at the last bloody moment.

Stilton from Paxton's as per. Selection of cottons, needles, zips and buttons as per. Rubber rings for kilner jars as per. Elizabeth Arden loose powder as per. Fine as per. But each year there was something she remembered at D-Day minus thirty seconds, something designed to make him go poling across town on some wild goose chase. Find another glass to replace the one that got broken – read, the one that you, Major Jacko Jackson, retired, or rather formerly retired but currently enduring court martial by the NAAFI, broke in a deliberate and malicious fashion after going heavy on the gargling juice. Vain to point out that it was the sort of glass which had gone out of stock even before we bought it second-hand. This year it was, Go to the big John Lewis on Oxford Street and see if they sell the outside bit of the salad spinner which sustained a life-threatening crack when it got dropped by Mister Someone, because the inside still works all right and they might just sell the outside bowl separately. And there in the car park she'd been waving the business part of it at him so that he could take it with him and not buy the wrong size or whatever. Practically trying to force it into his kitbag. Aagh.

Still, she made good coffee, he's always given her that. He set the flask on the table and unwrapped the foil package. Choccy biccies. Jacko's choccy biccies. He still thought of them like that. Was this right or wrong? Were you as young as you felt, or as old as you looked? That was the great question nowadays, it seemed to him. Maybe the only one. He poured himself some coffee and munched a biscuit. The soft, familiar, grey-green English landscape calmed him, then cheered him. Sheep, cattle, trees blown into hairstyles. A loitering canal. Put that canal on a charge, Sarnt-Major. Yes*sah*.

He was rather pleased with this year's postcard. A ceremonial sword in its scabbard. Subtle, that, he thought. Time was when he'd sent cards of field guns and famous Civil War battlefields. Well, he'd been younger then. Dear Babs, Dinner's on the 17th inst. Keep the afternoon free. Yours ever, Jacko. Quite straightforward. Never did anything like put it in an envelope. Principles of Concealment, section 5b, para 12: the enemy is seldom likely to spot anything placed directly in front of its face. He didn't even bother to go into Shrewsbury. Just bung the card in the village box.

Were you as young as you felt, or as old as you looked?
The ticket collector, or inspector, or train manager or whatever they called them nowadays, hadn't given him a glance.
Just saw a senior citizen's midweek excursion return and
read him as a piece of no trouble, no interest, some cheap-
skate who brought his own coffee as a way of saving money.
Well, that was true. The pension didn't stretch as far as it
had at first. He'd long ago given up his subscription to the
club. Apart from the annual regimental dinner, he only
needed to go up to town if his gnashers went wrong and
he didn't trust the local vet to fix them. Made far more sense
to stay in a b-and-b near the station. If you had the full works
for breakfast, managed to play your cards right and sneak
an extra sausage, you were set up for the day. Same again
on the Friday and that would get you through till you got
home. Back to base. Reporting for duty, all salad spinners
present and correct, *Ma'am*.

No, he wouldn't think of that yet. This was his annual
leave. His two days of furlough. He'd had his hair cut as
per. Had the blazer cleaned as per. He was an orderly man,
with orderly expectations and pleasures. Even if those pleasures were not as strong as they once had been. Different,
let's say. As you got older, your head for the sauce wasn't
what it used to be. You couldn't tie one on like in the old
days. So you drank less, enjoyed it more, and ended up just
as newted and owly as before. Well, that was the principle.
Didn't always work, of course. And the same with Babs.
How he remembered that first go-round, all those years ago.
Surprising he did, given his condition at the time. And that
was another thing, being newted and owly didn't seem to
make any difference to the honourable member then. Three
times. You old dog, Jacko. Once to say hullo; once the real
business; then once more for the road. Well, why else did
they sell rubber johnnies in packets of three? A week's supply

for some chaps, no doubt, but when you'd been saving it up as he had . . .

True, he could no longer tie one on like he used to. And the honourable member wasn't up to the three-card trick any more. Once was probably quite enough if you had your senior citizen's railcard. Wouldn't do to strain the ticker. And the idea of Pamela having to face something like that . . . No, he had no intention of straining the ticker. The ceremonial sword in its scabbard, and just a half-bottle of champagne between the two of them. They used to get through a whole bottle in the old days. Three glasses each, one for each go-round. Now it was just a half – something on special offer from that Thresher's near the station – and they often didn't finish it. Babs got heartburn easily and he didn't want to be too kiboshed for the regimental dinner. Mostly they talked. Sometimes they slept.

He didn't blame Pamela. Some women just went off it after the change. Simple matter of biology, nobody's fault. Just a question of female wiring. You set up a system, the system produces what it's designed for – namely, sprog-manufacture, witness Jennifer and Mike – and then shuts itself down. Old Mother Nature stops lubricating the parts. No surprise, given that Old Mother Nature is decidedly of the female persuasion. No one's to blame. So he wasn't to blame either. All he was doing was making sure *his* machinery was still in working order. Old Father Nature still lubricating the parts. A matter of hygiene, really.

Yes, that was right. He was straight with himself about it. No weasel words. Couldn't exactly discuss it with Pam, but as long as you could look yourself full in the shaving mirror. He wondered if those chaps he'd sat opposite at the dinner a couple of years ago could do that. The way they'd talked. A lot of the old mess rules had gone, of course, or were just ignored, and those little turkey-cocks had been pretty much rat-faced by the start of the dinner and had started maligning the fair sex before the port was passed. He'd have put them on a charge himself. The regiment had taken on a few too many clever-dicks lately, in his opinion. So he'd had to listen to the three of them holding forth as if the wisdom of the ages was at their beck and call. 'Marriage is a question of what you can get away with,' said the ringleader, and the others had nodded in agreement. This wasn't what had stuck in his craw, however. It was when the fellow had gone on to explain – or, more exactly, boast – how he'd taken up again with an old girlfriend, someone from back before he'd met his wife. 'Doesn't count,' one of the other clever-dicks had replied. 'Pre-existing adultery. Doesn't count.' Jacko had taken his while to work that one out, and when he did he didn't much like what he under-stood by it. Weasel words.

Had he been like that, back when he'd met Babs? No, he didn't think so. He didn't try and pretend things weren't what they were. He didn't say to himself, Oh it's because I was all newted and owly at the time, and, Oh it's because Pam is like she is nowadays. Nor did he say, Oh it's because Babs is blonde and I've always gone for blondes which is odd because Pam's a brunette unless of course it isn't odd at all. Babs was a nice girl, she was there, she was blonde, and they'd rung the gong three times that night. There wasn't more to it than that. Except that he'd remembered her. He'd remembered her, and the following year he'd found her again.

He spread his hand on the table before him. A hand-span plus an inch, that was the diameter of the salad spinner. Of course I'll remember, he'd told her: you don't think my hand's going to shrink in the next twenty-four hours, do you? No, don't put the guts in my kitbag, Pamela, I said I don't want to cart them up to town. Perhaps he could see how late John Lewis stayed open tonight. Call them from the station, pole over there this evening instead of tomorrow. That would save time. Then in the morning he could do all his other errands. Precision thinking, Jacko.

The following year he couldn't be sure Babs had remembered him, but even so she'd been pleased to see him. He'd brought a bottle of champagne on the off-chance, and that had somehow sealed things. He'd stayed the whole afternoon, told her about himself and they'd rung the gong three times again. He said he'd send her a postcard when he was up in town next, and that's how it had got going. And now it was – what? – twenty-two, twenty-three years? He'd brought her flowers on their tenth anniversary, a potted plant on their twentieth. A poinsettia. The thought of her kept him going on those bleak mornings when he went out to feed the pullets and scrape away at the coal bunker. She was – what was that phrase they used nowadays? – his window of opportunity. She'd tried to end it once – go into retirement, she'd joked – but he hadn't let her. He'd insisted, come close to making a scene. She'd given in, and stroked his face, and the next year when he'd sent his card he'd been scared fartless, but Babs had been as good as her word.

Of course they'd changed. Everyone changed. Pamela for a start: the children going, the garden, the thing she'd developed about dogs, the way she'd cut her hair as short as the lawn, the way she was always cleaning the house. Not that it seemed to him any different from how it had been before she started always cleaning it. And she'd stopped wanting to go anywhere, said she'd done her travelling. He'd said they had time on their hands nowadays; but they did and they didn't. They had more time and they got less done, that was the truth of the matter. And they weren't idle, either.

He'd changed, too. The way he found himself getting scared when he was up a ladder cleaning out the gutters. He'd done it for twenty-five years, for God's sake, it was top of his tasks list every spring, and with a bungalow you were never that far off the ground, but still he found himself scared. Not scared of falling off, it wasn't that. He always pushed down the side-locks on the ladder, he didn't suffer from vertigo, and he knew if he fell he'd probably land on grass. It was just that as he stood there, nose a few inches above the gutter, scraping at the moss and sodden leaves and stuff with a trowel, flicking out the twigs and bits of attempted bird's nest, looking up to check for broken tiles and see the TV aerial was still standing to attention – as he stood there, all protected, wellington boots on his feet, wind-cheater around him, woolly cap on his head and rubber gloves on his hands, he would sometimes feel the tears begin and he knew it wasn't because of the wind, and then he'd get stuck, one rubber hand clamped to the guttering, the other one pretending to poke in the curve of thick plastic, and he'd be scared fartless. Of the whole damn thing.

He liked to think that Babs never changed, and she didn't, not in his mind, not in his memory and his anticipation. But at the same time he acknowledged that her hair was no longer quite the blonde it had once been. And after he'd persuaded her not to go into retirement she'd changed too. Didn't like undressing in front of him. Kept her nightie on. Got heartburn from his champagne. One year he'd brought her the more expensive sort but the result was still the same. Turned out the light more and more. Didn't quite make the effort she once had to get him started. Slept when he slept; sometimes before.

But she was still what he looked forward to when he was feeding the pullets, scraping for coal, poking at the gutter with tears leaking, tears he smeared across his cheek-bones with the back of a rubber glove. She was his link to the past, to a past in which he could really tie one on and still ring the gong three times in a row. She could get a bit mumsy with him, but everyone needed that too, didn't they? Choccy biccy, Jacko? Yes, there was a bit of that. But also, you're a real man, you know that, Jacko? There aren't that many real men around, they're a dying breed, but you're one of them.

They were approaching Euston. A young chappie across from Jacko took out his bloody mobile phone and dialled pippily. 'Hello darling . . . yes, listen, bloody train's stuck somewhere outside bloody Birmingham. They don't tell you anything. No, at least an hour or more I'd say, and then I've got to get across London . . . Yes . . . Yes do that . . . Me too . . . Bye.' The liar tucked away his phone and stared around, daring anyone to have overheard.

So: run through the orders for the day again. Station, ring John Lewis re early strike on salad spinner. Dinner at one of those restaurants near the b-and-b: Indian, Turkish, didn't matter. Maximum expenditure £8. The Marquis of Granby, just the two pints, don't want to keep the billet awake with too many flushings in the night. Breakfast, extra sausage if poss. Half-bottle champagne from Thresher's. Errands for the NAAFI: stilton as per, kilner rings as per, loose powder as per. Two o'clock Babs. Two o'clock until six. Even the thought of it . . . Captain, art thou sleeping there below? Honourable members kindly rise . . . The ceremonial sword in its scabbard. Two until six. Tea at some point. Tea and a biccy. Funny how that had become part of the tradition too. And Babs was so good at encouraging a fellow, making him feel just for a moment, even in the dark, even with his eyes shut, just for a moment that he was . . . what he wanted to be.

'Right, that's it, me boy. Home, James, and don't spare the horses.' His kitbag was stowed between the seats, his mackintosh folded beside him. Ticket, wallet, sponge bag, tasks list now with little neat ticks appended. Rubber johnnies! That particular joke had been on him. The whole thing had been a joke on him. He did an eyes-right through the sealed window: an overlit sandwich bar, a stalled baggage-train, a porter in a silly uniform. Why do train drivers never have children? Because they always pull out on time. Ho bloody ho. Putting rubber johnnies on the list had always been his annual joke because he hadn't needed any. Not for years. Babs, once she knew and trusted him, said they didn't need to bother. He'd asked, what about the other thing, namely sprog-manufacture. She'd replied, 'Jacko, I think the danger of that's well past.'

It had all gone as per to begin with, per as in perfect. Train on time, pole across town to John Lewis, spread the hand to indicate gauge of salad spinner, size recognized, no spare parts alas sold separately, but special offer, probably cheaper now than when Madam bought it. Debate with self about whether to discard guts of salad spinner at point of purchase and claim he'd managed to locate and supply outer bowl by itself. Decision made to present whole item of *matériel* on return. After all, old Slippery Hands might celebrate one evening by dropping the insides of the thing for a change. Except that, knowing his luck, he'd probably smash the bowl again and they'd be stockpiling guts for the rest of their existence.

Back across town. Recognized and remembered by foreign chappie who ran the b-and-b. Coin in slot, report to base re safe arrival. Very decent chicken curry. Two pints, no more no less, at the Marquis of Granby. Discipline maintained. No undue pressure on bladder and prostate. Night surmounted with only the one visit to the latrines. Slept like the proverbial toddler. Sweet-talked way to extra sausage the next morning. Special offer on half of champagne at Thresher's. Tasks list accomplished with no hitch or glitch. Wash and brush-up, toothpaste duty. Presented self for inspection at two o'clock sharp.

And that was when the special offers ran out. He'd rung the bell picturing the familiar blonde curls and pink house-coat, hearing the giggles. But someone dark and artificial and middle-aged had answered the door. He stood there puzzled, not speaking.

'Present for me?' she'd said, probably just making conver-sation, and had reached out and taken the champagne by its neck. Instead of replying, he'd hung on to the bottle, and they had a silly tug-of-war until he said,

'Babs.'

'Babs'll be a little while,' she said, opening the door wider. This didn't seem right, but he followed her into the sitting-room which had been redecorated since this time last year. Redecorated like a whore's parlour, he'd thought.

'Shall I put that in the fridge?' she'd asked, but he held on to the bottle.

'Up from the country?' she'd asked.

'Military gentleman?' she'd asked.

'Cat got your tongue?' she'd asked.

They sat in silence for a quarter of an hour, until he heard one door close, then another. The dark-haired woman now stood in front of him with a tall blonde whose bra presented her titties to him like a fruit-bowl.

'Babs,' he'd repeated.

'I'm Babs,' the blonde replied.

'You're not Babs,' he'd said.

'If you say so,' she'd replied.

'You're not Babs,' he'd repeated.

The two women looked at one another, and the blonde had said, in a casual, hard way, 'Look, Grandpa, I'm whoever you want, right?'

He stood up. He looked at the two tarts. He explained,

slowly, so that even the most wet-eared recruit could understand.

'Oh,' one of them said. 'You mean Nora.'

'Nora?'

'Well, we called her Nora. I'm sorry. No, she passed on about nine months ago.'

He hadn't understood. He thought they meant she'd moved. Then he hadn't understood again. He thought they meant she'd been murdered, killed in a car crash, or something.

'She was rather elderly,' one of them said eventually, by way of explanation. He must have looked fierce, because she'd added, rather nervously, 'No offence. Nothing personal.'

They'd opened the champagne. The dark woman brought the wrong glasses. He and Babs had always drunk out of tumblers. The champagne was warm.

'I sent a postcard,' he said. 'A ceremonial sword.'

'Yes,' they answered, without interest.

They drained their glasses. The dark woman said, 'Well, do you still want what you've come for?'

He didn't exactly think about it. He must have nodded. The blonde girl said, 'Do you want me to be Babs?'

Babs had been Nora. That was what went through his brain. He felt himself grow fierce again. 'I want you to be what you are.' It was an order.

The two women looked at one another again. The blonde girl said, firmly but not convincingly, 'I'm Debbie.'

He should have left then. He should have left out of respect for Babs, out of loyalty to Babs.

On the other side of the sealed window the landscape went by, as it did every year, but he could find no shape in it. Sometimes he confused loyalty to Babs with loyalty to Pamela. He reached into his kitbag for the thermos.

Sometimes – oh, only a few times, but it had happened – he'd confused fucking Babs with fucking Pamela. It was as if he'd been at home. And as if that happened at home.

He'd gone into what used to be Babs's room. Redecorated too. He couldn't take in what was new, only what was missing from before. She'd asked him what he wanted. He hadn't replied. She'd taken some money and handed him a rubber johnny. He stood there holding it. Babs hadn't, Babs wouldn't . . .

'Want me to put it on for you, Gramps?'

He'd batted her hand away and dropped his trousers, then his pants. He knew he wasn't thinking well, but it seemed to be the best idea, the only idea. It was what he'd come for, after all. It was what he'd paid for now. The honourable member was temporarily hiding his light under a bushel, but if he indicated what was required, if he gave the orders, then . . . He sensed Debbie watching him, half-standing, one knee on the bed.

He squidgy-fingered the johnny onto his cock, expecting the action to bump-start it. He looked at Debbie, at the offered fruit-bowl, but that was no help. He looked down at his limp cock, at the wrinkled johnny with its drooping, unfillable teat. He felt the memory of lubricated rubber on his fingertips. He thought to himself, Right, that's it, me boy.

She had pulled a handful of tissues from the quilted box on the bedside table and handed them across. He dried his face. She gave him a little of his money back; just a little. He dressed quickly and walked out into the blinding streets. He wandered around pointlessly. A digital display above some shop told him it was three twelve. He realized the johnny was still on his cock.

Sheep. Cows. A tree blown into a hairstyle. A stupid bloody little encampment of bungalows full of stupid cunts who made him want to scream and puke and pull the alarm cord or whatever the fuck they had instead of the alarm cord nowadays. Stupid cunts just like himself. And he was going back to his own stupid bloody little bungalow that he'd spent so many years doing up. He unscrewed the thermos and poured himself some coffee. Two days in the flask and stone cold. In days of yore he used to liven it up with the contents of a hip flask. Now it was just cold, cold and old. Fair enough, eh, Jacko?

He'd have to give another coat of yacht varnish to the decking outside the French windows because it kept getting scuffed up by those new patio chairs . . . The utility room could do with a lick of paint . . . He'd take the mower in and have the blades sharpened, not that you could find anyone to do that nowadays, they just looked at you and suggested you bought one of those hover jobs with an orange plastic widget instead of a blade . . .

Babs was Nora. He didn't have to wear a johnny because she knew he didn't go anywhere else and she was way past getting pregnant. She only came out of retirement once a year, for his sake; just got a bit fond of you, Jacko, that's all. Made a joke one time about her bus pass and that was how he'd known she was older than him; older than Pam too. Once, when they were still getting through a whole bottle in the course of the afternoon, she'd offered to take her top teeth out to suck him, and he'd laughed but thought it disgusting. Babs was Nora and Nora was dead.

The fellows at dinner hadn't noticed any difference. He'd kept his discipline. Hadn't got rat-faced. 'Can't manage it so well any more, to tell the truth, old boy,' he had said, and someone had sniggered as if there was a joke in it. He'd bailed out early and had a drink at the Marquis of Granby. No, just the half tonight. Can't manage it so well any more, to tell the truth. Never say die, the barman had replied.

He despised himself for the way he'd pretended with that tart. Do you still want what you've come for? Oh yes, he still wanted what he'd come for, but that wasn't anything she could possibly know about. He and Babs hadn't done it for, what, five, six years? The last year or two they'd barely even sipped the champagne. He liked her to put on that mumsie nightie he was always teasing her about, climb into bed with him, turn out the light and talk about the old days. How it used to be. Once to say hullo, once the real business, once more for the road. You were a tiger in those days, Jacko. Quite wore me out. Used to take the next day off. You didn't. Oh yes I did. Well I never. Oh yes, Jacko, a real tiger.

She hadn't liked putting up her price, but rents were rents, and it was the space and the time he was paying for, whatever he wanted or didn't want to do. That was one thing about getting his senior citizen's railcard, he could save on the fare now. Not that there was a now any more. He'd seen the last of London. You could get Stilton and salad spinners in Shrewsbury, for God's sake. The regimental dinner would increasingly consist of seeing who wasn't there rather than who was. As for his teeth, the local vet could sort them out.

His packages were in the rack above him. His tasks list was a set of ticks. Pam would be on her way to the station by now, perhaps turning into the short-stay car park. Always went nose-first into a parking slot, did Pamela. Didn't like backing, preferred to save that for later; or, more likely, leave it for him to do. He was different. Preferred to back into the slot. That way you were ready for a quick departure. Just a matter of training, he supposed; keeping on the *qui vive*. Pamela used to say, when did we last need to make a quick departure? Anyway, there's usually a queue to get out. He used to say, if we got out first there wouldn't be a queue. Queue ED. And so on.

He promised himself he wouldn't look at the wheel-rims to see if she'd ground them down some more. He wouldn't pass any remarks as he wound down the window and reached across to the token-thingy. He wouldn't say, Look how far the wheels are away and I can still reach. He'd just ask, 'How are the dogs? Heard from the kids? Did they deliver the Super Dug?'

Yet he mourned Babs and he wondered if this was what it would be like to mourn Pamela. If it was that way round, of course.

He had done his tasks. As the train approached the station, he looked out of the sealed window, hoping to see his wife on the platform.

# THE REVIVAL

# I

# Petersburg

It was an old play of his, written in France back in 1849; promptly banned by the censor, and licensed for publication only in 1855. It first reached the stage seventeen years later, when it ran for a pitiful five nights in Moscow. Now, thirty years after its conception, she had telegraphed asking permission to abridge it for Petersburg. He agreed, while gently protesting that this juvenile invention had been meant for the page, not the stage. He added that the play was unworthy of her great talent. This was a typical gallantry: he had never seen her act.

Like most of his life's writing, the play was concerned with love. And as in his life, so in his writing: love did not work. Love might or might not provoke kindness, gratify vanity, and clear the skin, but it did not lead to happiness; there was always an inequality of feeling or intention present. Such was love's nature. Of course, it 'worked' in the sense that it caused life's profoundest emotions, made him fresh as spring's linden-blossom and broke him like a traitor on the wheel. It stirred him from well-mannered timidity to relative boldness, though a rather theoretical boldness, one tragicomically incapable of action. It taught him the gulping folly of anticipation, the wretchedness of failure, the whine of regret, and the silly fondness of remembrance. He knew love well. He also knew himself well. Thirty years earlier, he had written himself into the part of Rakitin, who offers the audience his conclusions about love: 'In my opinion, Alexei Nikolaevich, every love, happy as well as unhappy, is a real disaster when you give yourself over to it entirely.' These views were deleted by the censor.

He had assumed she would play the female lead, Natalya Petrovna, the married woman who falls in love with her son's tutor. Instead, she chose to be Natalya's ward Verochka, who, in the way of plays, also falls in love with the tutor. The production opened; he came to Petersburg; she called on him in his rooms at the Hotel de l'Europe. She had expected to be intimidated, but found herself charmed by the 'elegant and likeable grandpa' that she discovered. He treated her like a child. Was this so surprising? She was twenty-five, he was sixty.

On the 27th of March he went to a performance of his play. Despite hiding in the depths of the director's box, he was recognized, and at the end of the second act the audience started calling his name. She came to take him onstage; he refused, but took a bow from the box. After the next act, he went to her dressing-room, where he grasped her hands and examined her beneath the gaslight. 'Verochka,' he said. 'Have I really written this Verochka? I never paid her much attention when I was writing. The focal point of the play for me was Natalya Petrovna. But you are the living Verochka.'

# 2

# The Real Journey

So did he fall in love with his own creation? Verochka onstage beneath the floodlight, Verochka offstage beneath the gaslight, his Verochka, now prized the more for having been overlooked in his own text thirty years earlier? If love, as some assert, is a purely self-referring business, if the object of love is finally unimportant because what lovers value are their own emotions, then what more appropriate circularity than for a dramatist to fall in love with his own creation? Who needs the interference of the real person, the real *her* beneath the sunlight, the lamplight, the heartlight? Here is a photo of Verochka, dressed as for the schoolroom: timid and appealing, with ardour in her eyes and an open palm denoting trust.

But if this confusion occurred, she incited it. Years later, she wrote in her memoirs, 'I did not *play* Verochka, I performed a sacred rite . . . I felt quite distinctly that Verochka and I were the same person.' So we should be forgiving if 'the living Verochka' was what first moved him; what first moved her was perhaps something else that didn't exist – the author of the play, now himself long gone, thirty years away. And let's also remember that he knew this would be his last love. He was an old man now. He was applauded wherever he went as an institution, the representative of an era, someone whose work was done. Abroad, they hung gowns and ribbons on him. He was sixty, old by choice as well as fact. A year or two earlier, he had written: 'After the age of forty there is only one word to sum up the basis of life: *Renunciation.*' Now he was half as old again as that defining anniversary. He was sixty, she was twenty-five.

In letters, he kissed her hands, he kissed her feet. For her birthday, he sent a gold bracelet with their two names engraved inside. 'I feel now', he wrote, 'that I love you sincerely. I feel that you have become something in my life from which I shall never be parted.' The phrasing is conventional. Were they lovers? It seems not. For him, it was a love predicated upon renunciation, whose excitements were called if-only and what-might-have-been.

But all love needs a journey. All love symbolically is a journey, and that journey needs bodying forth. *Their* journey took place on the 28th of May 1880. He was staying on his country estate; he pressed her to visit him there. She couldn't: she was an actress, at work, on tour; even she had things that must be renounced. But she would be travelling from Petersburg to Odessa; her route could take her through Mtsensk and Oryol. He consulted the timetable for her. Three trains left Moscow along the Kursk line. The 12.30, the 4 o'clock, and the 8.30: the express, the mail, and the slow train. Respective arrivals at Mtsensk: 10 in the evening, 4.30 in the morning, and 9.45 in the morning. There was the practicality of romance to be considered. Should the beloved arrive with the post, or on the railway's equivalent of the red-eye? He urged her to take the 12.30, redefining its arrival more exactly to 9.55 p.m.

There is an ironic side to this precision. He was himself notoriously unpunctual. At one time, affectedly, he carried a dozen watches on his person; even so, he would be hours late for a rendezvous. But on May the 28th, trembling like a youth, he met the 9.55 express at the little station of Mtsensk. Night had fallen. He boarded the train. It was thirty miles from Mtsensk to Oryol.

He sat in her compartment for those thirty miles. He gazed

at her, he kissed her hands, he inhaled the air she exhaled. He did not dare to kiss her lips: renunciation. Or, he tried to kiss her lips and she turned her face away: embarrassment, humiliation. The banality too, at his age. Or, he kissed her and she kissed him back as ardently: surprise, and leaping fear. We cannot tell: his diary was later burned, her letters have not survived. All we have are his subsequent letters, whose gauge of reliability is that they date this May journey to the month of June. We know that she had a travelling companion, Raisa Alexeyevna. What did she do? Feign sleep, pretend to have sudden night vision for the darkened landscape, retreat behind a volume of Tolstoy? Thirty miles passed. He got off the train at Oryol. She sat at her window, waving her handkerchief to him as the express took her on towards Odessa.

No, even that handkerchief is invented. But the point is, they had had their journey. Now it could be remembered, improved, turned into the embodiment, the actuality of the if-only. He continued to invoke it until his death. It was, in a sense, his last journey, the last journey of the heart. 'My life is behind me,' he wrote, 'and that hour spent in the railway compartment, when I almost felt like a twenty-year-old youth, was the last burst of flame.'

Does he mean he almost got an erection? Our knowing age rebukes its predecessor for its platitudes and evasions, its sparks, its flames, its fires, its imprecise scorchings. Love isn't a bonfire, for God's sake, it's a hard cock and a wet cunt, we growl at these swooning, renouncing people. Get on with it! Why on earth didn't you? Cock-scared, cunt-bolted tribe of people! *Hand*-kissing! It's perfectly obvious what you really wanted to kiss. So why not? And on a train too. You'd just have to hold your tongue in place and let the movement of the train do the work for you. Clackety-clack, clackety-clack!

When did you last have your hands kissed? And if you

did, how do you know he was any good at it? (Further, when did anyone last *write* to you about kissing your hands?) Here is the argument for the world of renunciation. If we know more about consummation, they knew more about desire. If we know more about numbers, they knew more about despair. If we know more about boasting, they knew more about memory. They had foot-kissing, we have toe-sucking. You still prefer our side of the equation? You may well be right. Then try a simpler formulation: if we know more about sex, they knew more about love.

Or perhaps this is quite wrong, and we mistake the gradations of courtly style for realism. Perhaps foot-kissing always meant toe-sucking. He also wrote to her: 'I kiss your little hands, your little feet, kiss everything you will allow me to kiss, and even that which you will not.' Isn't this clear enough, to both writer and recipient? And if so, then perhaps the converse is also true: that heart-reading was just as coarsely practised then as it is now.

But as we mock these genteel fumblers of a previous era, we should prepare ourselves for the jeers of a later century. How come we never think of that? We believe in evolution, at least in the sense of evolution culminating in us. We forget that this entails evolution beyond our solipsistic selves. Those old Russians were good at dreaming a better time, and idly we claim their dreams as our applause.

While her train continued towards Odessa, he spent the night at a hotel in Oryol. A bipolar night, splendid in his thoughts of her, miserable because this prevented him from sleeping. The voluptuousness of renunciation was now upon him. 'I find my lips murmuring, "What a night we should have spent together!"' To which our practical and irritated century replies, 'Take another train then! Try kissing her wherever it was you didn't!'

Such action would be far too dangerous. He must

preserve the impossibility of love. So he offers her an extravagant if-only. He confesses that as her train was about to leave he was suddenly tempted by the 'madness' of abducting her. It was a temptation he typically renounced: 'The bell rang, and *ciao*, as the Italians say.' But think of the newspaper headlines if he had carried out his momentary plan. 'SCANDAL AT ORYOL RAILWAY STATION,' he delightedly imagines to her. If only. 'An extraordinary event took place here yesterday: the author T—, an elderly man, was accompanying the celebrated actress S—, who was travelling to Odessa for a brilliant season in the theatre there, when, just as the train was about to pull out, he, as though possessed by the Devil in person, extracted Madame S—through the window of her compartment and, overcoming the artiste's desperate efforts, etc., etc.' If only. The real moment – the possible handkerchief being waved at the window, the probable station gaslight falling on the whitened crest of an old man – is rewritten into farce and melodrama, into journalese and 'madness'. The alluring hypothetical does not refer to the future; it is safely lodged in the past. The bell rang, and *ciao*, as the Italians say.

He also had another tactic: that of hurrying on into the future in order to confirm the impossibility of love in the present. Already, and without 'anything' having happened, he is looking back on this would-have-been something. 'If we meet again in another two or three years, I shall be an old, old man. As for you, you will have entered definitively upon the normal course of your life and nothing will remain of our past . . .' Two years, he thought, would turn an old man into an old, old one; while 'normal life' is already waiting for her in the banal yet timely shape of an officer of hussars, clanking his spurs offstage and snorting like a horse. N. N. Vsevolozhsky. How useful the thunderous uniform was to the gauntly bent civilian.

We should not, by this point, still be thinking of Verochka, the naïve, unfortunate ward. The actress who embodied her was robust, temperamental, bohemian. She was already married, and seeking a divorce to acquire her hussar; she would marry three times in all. Her letters have not survived. Did she lead him on? Was she a little in love with him? Was she, perhaps, more than a little in love with him, yet dismayed by his expectation of failure, his voluptuous renunciations? Did she, perhaps, feel just as trapped by his past as he did? If love for him had always meant defeat, why should it be any different with her? If you marry a foot-fetishist, you shouldn't be surprised to find him curled up in your shoe-cupboard.

When he recalled that journey in letters to her, he made oblique references to the word 'bolt'. Was this the lock on the compartment, on her lips, on her heart? Or the lock on his flesh? 'You know what the predicament of Tantalus was?' he wrote. The predicament of Tantalus was to be tortured in the infernal regions by endless thirst; he was up to his neck in water, but whenever he bent his head to drink, the river would run away from him. Are we to conclude from this that he tried to kiss her, but that whenever he advanced, she retreated, withdrawing her wet mouth?

On the other hand, a year later, when everything is safe and stylized, he writes this: 'You say, at the end of your letter, "I kiss you warmly". How? Do you mean, as you did then, on that June night, in the railway compartment? If I live a hundred years I will never forget those kisses.' May has become June, the timid suitor has become the recipient of myriad kisses, the bolt has been slid back a little. Is this the truth, or is that the truth? We, now, would like it to be neat then, but it is rarely neat; whether the heart drags in sex, or sex drags in the heart.

# 3

# The Dream Journey

He travelled. She travelled. But *they* did not travel; never again. She visited him at his estate, she swam in his pond – 'the Undine of Saint Petersburg' he called her – and when she left he named the room in which she had slept after her. He kissed her hands, he kissed her feet. They met, they corresponded until his death, after which she protected his memory from vulgar interpretation. But thirty miles was all they travelled together.

They could have travelled. If only . . . if only.

But he was a connoisseur of the if-only, and so they did travel. They travelled in the past conditional.

She was about to marry for the second time. N. N. Vsevolozhsky, officer of hussars, clank, clank. When she asked his opinion of her choice, he declined to play. 'It is too late to ask for my opinion. *Le vin est tiré – il faut le boire.*' Was she asking him, artist to artist, for his view of the conventional marriage she was about to make to a man with whom she had little in common? Or was it more than this? Was she proposing her own if-only, asking him to sanction the jilting of her fiancé?

But Grandpa, who himself had never married, declines either to sanction or applaud. *Le vin est tiré – il faut le boire.* Does he have a habit of lapsing into foreign phrases at key emotional moments? Do French and Italian provide the suave euphemisms which helps him evade?

Of course, if he had encouraged a late withdrawal from her second marriage, that would have let in too much reality, let in the present tense. He closes it off: drink the wine. This instruction given, fantasy can resume. In his next letter, twenty days later, he writes, 'For my part, I am dreaming about how good it would be to travel about – just the two of us – for at least a month, and in such a way that no one would know who or where we were.'

It is a normal dream of escape. Alone together, anonymous, time on one's hands. It is also, of course, a honeymoon. And where would the sophisticated artistic class go for their honeymoon if not to Italy? 'Just imagine the following picture,' he teases. 'Venice (perhaps in October, the best month in Italy) or Rome. Two foreigners in travelling clothes – one tall, clumsy, white-haired, long-legged, but very contented; the other a slender lady with remarkable dark eyes and black hair. Let us suppose her contented as well. They walk about the town, ride in gondolas. They visit galleries, churches, and so on, they dine together in the evening, they are at the theatre together – and then? There my imagination stops respectfully. Is it in order to conceal something, or because there is nothing to conceal?'

Did his imagination stop respectfully? Ours doesn't. It seems pretty plain to us in our subsequent century. A crumbling gentleman in a crumbling city on a surrogate honeymoon with a young actress. The gondoliers are splish-sploshing them back to their hotel after an intimate supper, the soundtrack is operetta, and we need to be told what happens next? We are not talking about reality, so the feebleness of elderly, alcohol-weakened flesh is not an issue; we are very safely in the conditional tense, with the travelling rug tucked round us. So . . . if only . . . if only . . . then you would have fucked her, wouldn't you? No denying it.

Elaborating the Venice honeymoon fantasy with a woman still between husbands has its dangers. Of course, you have again renounced her, so there is small risk that by exciting her imagination you might find her outside your front door one morning, perched on a travelling trunk and coyly fanning herself with her passport. No: the more real danger is of pain. Renunciation means the avoidance of love, and hence of pain, but even in this avoidance there are traps. There is pain to be had, for instance, in the comparison between the Venetian capriccio of your respectful imagination and the impending reality of her getting disrespectfully fucked on her actual honeymoon by an officer of hussars, N. N. Vsevolozhsky, who is as unfamiliar with the Accademia as he is with the unreliabilities of the flesh.

What heals pain? Time, the old wiseacres respond. You know better. You are wise enough to know that time does not always heal pain. The conventional image of the amatory bonfire, the eyeball-drying flame which dies to sad ashes, needs adjusting. Try instead a hissing gas-jet that scorches if you will but also does worse: it gives light, jaundicing, flat-shadowed and remorseless, the sort of light that catches an old man on a provincial platform as the train pulls out, a valetudinarian who watches a yellow window and a twitching hand withdraw from his life, who walks after the train a few paces as it curves into invisibility, who fixes his eye upon the red lamp of the guard's wagon, holds on that until it is less than a ruby planet in the night sky, then turns away and finds himself still beneath a platform lamp, alone, with nothing to do except wait out the hours in a musty hotel, convincing himself he has won while knowing truly that he has lost, filling his sleeplessness with cosy if-onlies, and then return to the station and stand alone once more, in a kinder light but to make a crueller journey, back along those thirty miles he had travelled with her the previous night. The passage from Mtsensk to Oryol, which he will commemorate for the rest of his life, is always shadowed by that unrecorded return from Oryol to Mtsensk.

So he proposes a second dream journey, again to Italy. By now she is married, a change of status which is not an interesting subject for discussion. Drink the wine. She is going to Italy, perhaps with her husband, though travelling companions are not enquired after. He approves the journey, if only because it lets him offer her an alternative; not a rivalrous honeymoon this time, but a trip back in the painless past conditional. 'I spent ten of the most delightful days in Florence, many, many years ago.' This use of time anaesthetizes pain. It was so many, many years ago that he was then 'still under forty' – before the basis for life became renunciation. 'Florence left on me the most fascinating and poetic impression – even though I was there *alone*. What it would have been like, had I been in the company of a woman who was understanding, good and beautiful – that above all!'

This is safe. The fantasy is manageable, his gift a false memory. A few decades later, the political leaders of his country would specialize in airbrushing the downfallen from history, in removing their photographic traces. Now here he is, bent over his album of memories, meticulously inserting the figure of a past companion. Paste it in, that photograph of the timid, appealing Verochka, while the lamplight rejuvenates your white hair into black shadow.

# 4

# At Yasnaya Polyana

Shortly after meeting her, he had gone to stay with Tolstoy, who took him out shooting. He was put in the best hide, over which snipe habitually passed. But that day, for him, the sky remained empty. Every so often, a shot would ring out from Tolstoy's hide; then another; then another. All the snipe were flying to Tolstoy's gun. It seemed typical. He himself shot a single bird, which the dogs failed to find.

Tolstoy thought him ineffectual, vacillating, unmanly, a frivolous socializer and a despicable Westernizer; embraced him, loathed him, spent a week in Dijon with him, quarrelled with him, forgave him, valued him, visited him, challenged him to a duel, embraced him, scorned him. This is how Tolstoy expressed sympathy when he lay dying in France: 'The news of your illness has caused me much sorrow, especially when I was assured it was serious. I realized how much I cared for you. I felt that I should be much grieved if you were to die before me.'

Tolstoy at this time despised the taste for renunciation. Later, he began railing at the lusts of the flesh and idealizing a Christian peasant simplicity. His attempts at chastity failed with comic frequency. Was he a fraud, a fake renunciator; or was it more that he lacked the skills, and his flesh declined renunciation? Three decades later he died on a railway station. His last words were not, 'The bell rang, and *ciao*, as the Italians say.' Does the successful renunciator envy his unsuccessful counterpart? There are ex-smokers who decline the offered cigarette but say, 'Blow the smoke in my direction.'

She was travelling; she was working; she was married. He asked her to send him a plaster cast of her hand. He had kissed the real thing so many times, kissed an imagined version of the real thing in almost every letter he wrote her. Now he could lay his lips on a plaster version. Is plaster nearer to flesh than air? Or did the plaster turn his love and her flesh into a memorial? There is an irony to his request: normally it is the writer whose creative hand is cast in plaster; and normally by the time this is done he is dead.

So he proceeded deeper into old age, knowing that she was – had already been – his last love. And since form was his business, did he at this time remember his first love? He was a specialist in the matter. Did he reflect that first love fixes a life for ever? Either it impels you to repeat the same kind of love and fetishizes its components; or else it is there as warning, trap, counter-example.

His own first love had taken place fifty years before. She had been a certain Princess Shakhovskaya. He was fourteen, she was in her twenties; he adored her, she treated him like a child. This puzzled him until the day he found out why. She was already his father's mistress.

The year after he shot snipe with Tolstoy, he visited Yasnaya Polyana again. It was Sonya Tolstoy's birthday, and the house was full of guests. He proposed that each of them should recount the happiest moment of their lives. When his own turn in his own game arrived, he announced, with an exalted air and a familiar melancholy smile: 'The happiest moment of my life is, of course, the moment of love. It is the moment when you meet the eyes of the woman you love and sense that she loves you too. This has happened to me once, perhaps twice.' Tolstoy found this answer irritating.

Later, when the young people insisted upon dancing, he demonstrated what was new in Paris. He took off his jacket, stuck his thumbs in the armholes of his waistcoat and capered about, legs kicking, head waggling, white hair flopping, as the household clapped and cheered; he panted, capered, panted, capered, then fell over and collapsed into an armchair. It was a great success. Tolstoy wrote in his journal: 'Turgenev – can-can. Sad.'

'Once, perhaps twice.' Was she the 'perhaps twice'? Perhaps. In his penultimate letter, he kisses her hands. In his last letter, written in failing pencil, he does not offer kisses. He writes instead: 'I do not change in my affections – and I shall keep exactly the same feeling for you until the end.'

This end came six months later. The plaster cast of her hand is now in the Theatre Museum of Saint Petersburg, the city where he had first kissed the original.

# VIGILANCE

It all started when I poked the German. Well, he might have been Austrian – it was Mozart after all – and it didn't really start then, but years before. Still, it's best to give a specific date, don't you think?

So: a Thursday in November, the Royal Festival Hall, 7.30 p.m., Mozart K595 with Andras Schiff, followed by Shostakovich 4. I remember thinking as I set off that the Shostakovich had some of the loudest passages in the history of music, and you certainly wouldn't be able to hear anything over the top of *them*. But this is jumping ahead. 7.29 p.m.: the hall was full, the audience normal. The last people to arrive were strolling in from a sponsor's pre-concert drinks downstairs. You know the sort – oh, it seems to be about half-past, but let's just finish this glass, have a pee, then saunter upstairs and barge past half a dozen people on the way to our seats. Take your time, pal: the boss is putting up some moolah, so Maestro Haitink can always hang on a bit longer in the green room.

The Austro-German – to give him his due – had at least arrived by 7.23 p.m. He was smallish, baldish, with glasses, a sticky-up collar and red bow-tie. Not exactly evening dress; perhaps some going-out gear typical of where he came from. And he was pretty bumptious, I thought, not least because he had two women in tow, one on either side. They were all in their mid-thirties, I'd say: old enough to know better. 'These are good seats,' he announced, as they found their places in front of me. J 37, 38 and 39. I was in K 37. I instantly took against him. Praising himself to his escorts for the tickets he'd bought. I suppose he could have got them from an agency, and was just relieved; but he didn't say it like that. And why give him the benefit of the doubt?

As I say, it was a normal audience. Eighty per cent on day release from the city's hospitals, with pulmonary wards and ear-nose-and-throat departments getting ticket priority. Book now for a better seat if you have a cough which comes in at more than 95 decibels. At least people don't fart in concerts. I've never heard anyone fart, anyway. Have you? I expect they do. Which is partly my point: if you can suppress at one end, why not at the other? You get roughly the same amount of warning in my experience. But people don't on the whole fart raucously in Mozart. So I suppose a few vestiges of the thin crust of civilization which prevents our descent into utter barbarism are just about holding.

The opening *allegro* went pretty well: a couple of sneezes, a bad case of compacted phlegm in the middle of the terrace which nearly required surgical intervention, one digital watch and a fair amount of programme turning. I sometimes think they ought to put directions for use on the cover of programmes. Like: 'This is a programme. It tells you about tonight's music. You might like to glance at it before the concert begins. Then you will know what is being played. If you leave it too late, you will cause visual distraction and a certain amount of low-level noise, you will miss some of the music, and risk annoying your neighbours, especially the man in seat K 37.' Occasionally a programme will contain a small piece of information, vaguely bordering on advice, about mobile phones, or the use of a handkerchief to cough into. But does anyone pay any heed? It's like smokers reading the health warning on a packet of cigarettes. They take it in and they don't take it in; at some level, they don't believe it applies to them. It must be the same with coughers. Not that I want to sound too understanding: that way lies forgiveness. And on a point of information, how often do you actually see a muffling handkerchief come out? I was at the back of the stalls once, T 21. The Bach double concerto. My neighbour, T 20, suddenly began rearing up as if athwart a bronco. With pelvis thrust forward, he delved frantically for his handkerchief, and managed to hook out at the same time a large bunch of keys. Distracted by their fall, he let handkerchief and sneeze go off in separate directions. Thank you very much, T 20. Then he spent half the slow movement eyeing his keys anxiously. Eventually he solved the problem by putting his foot over them and contentedly returning his gaze to the soloists. From time to time a faint metallic stir from beneath his shifting shoe added some useful gracenotes to Bach's score.

The *allegro* ended, and Maestro Haitink slowly lowered his head, as if giving everyone permission to use the spitoon and talk about their Christmas shopping. J 39 – the Viennese blonde, a routine programme-shuffler and hair-adjuster – found a lot to say to Mr Sticky-Up Collar in J 38. He was nodding away in agreement about the price of pullovers or something. Maybe they were discussing Schiff's delicacy of touch, though I would choose to doubt it. Haitink raised his head to indicate that it was time for the chat-line to go off air, lifted his stick to demand an end to coughing, then threw in that subtle, cocked-ear half-turn to indicate that he, personally, for one, was now intending to listen very carefully indeed to the pianist's entry. The *larghetto*, as you probably know, begins with the unsupported piano announcing what those who had bothered to read the programme would have known to expect as a 'simple, tranquil melody'. This is also the concerto in which Mozart decided to do without trumpets, clarinets and drums: in other words, we are being invited to attend to the piano even more closely. And so, with Haitink's head staying cocked, and Schiff offering us the first few tranquil bars, J 39 remembered what she hadn't finished saying about pullovers.

I leaned across and poked the German. Or the Austrian. I've nothing against foreigners, by the way. Admittedly, if he'd been a vast, burger-fed Brit in a World Cup t-shirt, I might have thought twice. And in the case of the Austro-German, I did think twice. Like this. One: you're coming to hear music in *my* country, so don't behave as if still in yours. Then two: given where you probably come from, it's even worse to behave like this in Mozart. So I poked J 38 with a joined tripod of thumb and first two fingers. Hard. He turned instinctively, and I glared at him with finger tapping my lips. J 39 stopped chattering, J 38 looked gratifyingly guilty, and J 37 looked a bit scared. K 37 – me – went back to the music. Not that I could entirely concentrate on it. I felt jubilation rising in me like a sneeze. At last I'd done it, after all these years.

When I got home, Andrew applied his usual logic in an attempt to deflate me. Perhaps my victim thought it OK to behave as he did because everyone around him was doing the same; it wasn't unmannerly but an attempt to be mannerly – *wenn in London* . . . Additionally and alternatively, Andrew wanted to know, wasn't it the case that much music of that time was composed for royal or ducal courts, and wouldn't such patrons and their retinue have been strolling around, having a buffet supper, throwing chicken bones at the harpist, and flirting with their neighbours' wives while half-listening to their lowly employee bash away at the spinet? But the music wasn't composed with bad behaviour in mind, I protested. How do you know, Andrew replied: surely those composers were aware of how their music was going to be listened to, and either wrote music loud enough to cover the noise of chicken-bone-throwing and general eructation, or, more likely, tried to write tunes of such commanding beauty that even a lustful upcountry baronet would for a moment stop tampering with the exposed flesh of the apothecary's wife? Was this not the challenge – indeed, perhaps the reason why the resultant music had lasted so long and so well? Furthermore and finally, this harmless neighbour of mine in the wing-collar was quite possibly a linear descendant of that upcountry baronet, simply behaving in the same way: he'd paid his money and was entitled to listen to as much or as little as he chose.

'In Vienna,' I said, 'twenty or thirty years ago, when you went to the opera, if you uttered the slightest cough, a flunky in knee-breeches and a powdered wig would come over and give you a cough-sweet.'

'That must have distracted people even more.'

'It stopped them doing it the next time.'

'Anyway, I don't understand why you still go to concerts.'

'For the good of my health, doctor.'

'It seems to be having the opposite effect.'

'No one's going to stop me going to concerts,' I said. 'No one.'

'We don't talk about that,' he replied, looking away.

'I wasn't talking about it.'

'Good.'

Andrew thinks I should stay at home with my sound system, my collection of CDs, and our tolerant neighbours who are very rarely heard clearing their throats on the other side of the party wall. Why bother going to concerts, he asks, when it only enrages you? I bother, I tell him, because when you are in a concert hall, having paid money and taken the trouble to go there, you listen more carefully. Not from what you tell me, he answers: you seem to be distracted most of the time. Well, I would pay more attention if I wasn't being distracted. And what would you pay more attention to, as a purely theoretical question (you see how provoking Andrew can be)? I thought about this for a while, then said: the loud bits and the soft bits, actually. The loud bits, because however state-of-the-art your system, nothing can compare to the reality of a hundred or more musicians going full tilt in front of you, cramming the air with noise. And the soft bits, which is more paradoxical, because you'd think any hi-fi could reproduce them well enough. But it can't. For instance, those opening bars of the *larghetto*, floating across twenty, thirty, fifty yards of space; though floating isn't the right word, because it implies time spent travelling, and when the music is on its way towards you, all sense of time is abolished, as is space, and place, for that matter.

'So how was the Shostakovich? Loud enough to drown the bastards out?'

'Well,' I said, 'that's an interesting point. You know how it starts off with those huge climaxes? It made me realize what I meant about the loud bits. Everyone was making as much noise as possible – brass, timps, big bad drum – and you know what cut through it all? The xylophone. There was this woman bashing away and coming across clear as a bell. Now, if you'd heard that on a record you'd think it was the result of some fancy bit of engineering – spot-lighting, or whatever they call it. In the hall you knew that this was just exactly what Shostakovich intended.'

'So you had a good time?'

'But it also made me realize that it's the pitch that counts. The piccolo cuts through in the same way. So it's not just the cough or the sneeze and its volume, but the musical texture it's competing with. Which means of course you can't relax even in the loudest bits.'

'Cough-sweets and a powdered wig for you,' said Andrew. 'Otherwise, you know, I think you'll go seriously, woofingly mad.'

'Coming from you,' I replied.

He knew what I meant. Let me tell you about Andrew. We've lived together for twenty or more years now; we met in our late thirties. He works in the furniture department of the V & A. Cycles there every day, rain or shine; one side of London to the other. On his way he does two things: listens to books on tape with his Walkman, and keeps an eye out for firewood. I know, it doesn't sound likely, but most days he manages to fill his basket, enough for an evening fire. So he pedals along from this one civilized place to another, listening to cassette 325 of *Daniel Deronda*, while constantly on the lookout for skips and fallen branches.

But that's not all. Even though Andrew knows a lot of cut-throughs where the firewood hangs out, he spends more than enough of the journey in rush-hour traffic. And you know what motorists are like: they only look out for other motorists. Buses and lorries as well, of course; motor-cyclists occasionally; pedal-cyclists, never. And this makes Andrew hopping mad. There they are, sitting on their arses, pouring out fumes, one person to a car, a traffic-jam of environmentally abusive egoists constantly trying to swerve into an eighteen-inch gap without first checking for the presence of cyclists. Andrew shouts at them. Andrew, my civilized friend, companion and ex-lover, Andrew, who has spent half the day bent over some exquisite piece of marquetry with a restorer, Andrew, his ears full of high-Victorian sentences, breaks off to shout,

'You fucking cunt!'

He also shouts, 'I hope you get cancer!'

Or, 'Drive under a fucking lorry, arse-face!'

I ask what he says to women drivers.

'Oh, I don't call them cunts,' he replies. '"You fucking bitch!" usually seems to cover it.'

Then off he pedals, scouting for firewood and worrying

about Gwendolen Harleth. He used to bang on car roofs
when a driver cut him up. Bang bang bang with a sheep-
skin-lined glove. It must have sounded like a thunder-
machine from Strauss or Henze. He also used to snap their
wing-mirrors back, folding them in against the car; that used
to irritate the bastards. But he's stopped doing this; about a
year ago he had a scare from a blue Mondeo which caught
up with him and tipped him off the bike while the driver
made various threatening suggestions. Now he just calls
them fucking cunts at the top of his voice. They can't object,
because that's what they are, and they know it.

I started taking cough-sweets to concerts. I handed them
out like spot fines to offenders within my immediate reach,
and to distant hackers at the interval. It wasn't a great
success, as I might have foreseen. If you give someone a
wrapped sweet in the middle of a concert, you then have
to listen to the sound of them taking the paper off. And if
you give them one unwrapped, they're hardly likely to just
pop it into their mouths, are they?

Some people even failed to realize I was being offensive,
or retaliatory; they actually thought it was a friendly gesture.
And then one evening I stopped that boy near the bar, put
my hand on his elbow, but not hard enough for the gesture
to be unambiguous. He turned, black turtleneck sweater,
leather jacket, spiky blond hair, broad, virtuous face. Swedish
perhaps, Danish, maybe a Finn. He looked at what I was
holding out towards him.

'My mother always told me never to take sweets from
kind gentlemen,' he said with a smile.

'You were coughing,' I replied, feebly unable to sound
cross.

'Thank you.' He took the sweet by the wrapper end,
and gently tugged it away from my fingers. 'Would you like
a drink?'

No, no, I wouldn't like a drink. Why not? For the reason we don't talk about. I was on those side-stairs down from level 2A. Andrew had gone for a pee and I got talking to this boy. I thought I had more time. We were just exchanging numbers when I turned and Andrew was watching. I could hardly pretend I was buying a second-hand car. Or that this was the first time. Or that . . . anything, really. We didn't go back for the second half (Mahler 4) and instead had a long bad evening of it. And that was the last time Andrew came to a concert with me. He stopped wanting to share my bed as well. He said he'd still (probably) love me, still (probably) live with me, but he didn't ever want to fuck me again. And later he said he didn't even want anything halfway to fucking either, thank you very much. Perhaps you'd think this would make me say Yes please, I would like a drink, to the smiley, virtuous-faced Swede or Finn or whatever. But you'd be wrong. No, I wouldn't, thank you, no.

It's hard to get it right, isn't it? And it must be the same for the performers. If they ignore the bronchitic bastards out there, they risk giving the impression that they're so engrossed in the music that, hey, cough away as much as you like and they won't notice. But if they attempt to impose their authority . . . I've seen Brendel turn away from the keyboard in the middle of a Beethoven sonata and glare outwards in the rough direction of the offender. But the bastard probably doesn't even notice he's being rebuked, while the rest of us start fretting about whether or not Brendel's been put off, and so on.

I decided on a new approach. The cough-sweet approach was like an ambiguous gesture from cyclist to motorist: yes, thank you kindly for swerving across the lanes, I was planning to jam my brakes on and have a heart attack anyway. None of that. Perhaps it was time to bang on their roofs a little.

Let me explain that I am of reasonably sturdy physique: two decades in the gym haven't done me any harm; compared to the average pigeon-chested concert-goer I might be a lorry-driver. Also, I dressed myself in a dark blue suit of a thick, sergey material; white shirt; dark blue un-decorated tie; and in my lapel a badge with a heraldic shield. I pitched the effect deliberately. A malefactor might well mistake me for an official usher. Finally, I moved from the stalls to the annex. That's the section running along the side of the auditorium: from there you can follow the conductor while also policing the stalls and the front half of the terrace. This usher would not hand out cough-sweets. This usher would wait until the interval, and then follow the offender – in as ostentatious a way as possible – out to the bar, or one of those undifferentiated areas with wide-screen views of the Thames skyline.

'Excuse me, sir, but are you aware of the decibel-level of the unmuffled cough?'

They would look at me rather nervously, as I made sure that my voice was also unmuffled. 'It's reckoned at about 85,' I would continue. 'A fortissimo note on the trumpet is about the same.' I quickly learnt not to give them the chance to explain how they'd picked up that nasty throat, and would never do it again, or whatever. 'So, thank you, sir, we would be grateful . . .' And I moved on, that *we* lingering as endorse-ment of my quasi-official status.

With women I was different. There is, as Andrew pointed out, a necessary distinction between You fucking cunt and You fucking bitch. And there was often the problem of the male companion or husband who might feel within himself stirrings from the time when caves were daubed with ruddy bison in stylish freehand. 'We *do* sympathize about the cough, madam,' I would say, in a lowered, almost medical voice, 'but the orchestra and conductor find it quite unhelpful.' This was, when they came to consider it, even more offensive; more the snapped-back mirror than the thundered roof.

But I also wanted to bang on the roof. I wanted to be offensive. It seemed right. So I developed various lines of abuse. For instance, I would identify the malefactor, follow him (statistically it usually was a him) to where he was standing with his interval coffee or half of lager, and ask, in what therapists would call a non-confrontational manner, 'Excuse me, but do you like art? Do you go to museums and galleries?'

This generally produced a positive response, even if one tinged with suspicion. Might I have a hidden clipboard and questionnaire? So I would quickly follow up my initial question. 'And what would you say is your favourite painting? One of them, anyway?'

People like being asked this, and I might be rewarded with The Hay Wain or The Rokeby Venus or Monet's Water Lilies or whatever.

'Well, imagine this,' I'd say, all polite and cheerful. 'You're standing in front of The Rokeby Venus, and I'm standing next to you, and while you're looking at it, at this incredibly famous picture which you love more than anything else in the world, I start gobbing on it, so that bits of the canvas are all covered in spit. I don't just do it once, but several times. What would you think about that?' I am maintaining my reasonable-man-not-quite-with-clipboard tone.

The answers vary between proposed action and reflection, between 'I'd call the guards' and 'I'd think you were a nutter.'

'Exactly,' I reply, moving a little closer. 'So *don't*' – and here I sometimes give them a poke in the shoulder or on the chest, a poke which is a little harder than they expect –

'*don't* cough in the middle of Mozart. It's like gobbing on The Rokeby Venus.'

Most look sheepish at this point, and a few have the decency to react as if they've been caught shoplifting. One or two say, 'Who do you think you are?' To which I reply, 'Just someone who's paid for his seat like you.' Note that I never claim to be an official. Then I add: 'And I'll be keeping an eye on you.'

Some of them lie. 'It's hay fever,' they say, and I answer, 'Bring the hay in with you, did you?' One studenty type was apologetic about his timing: 'I thought I knew the piece. I thought there was a sudden crescendo, not a diminuendo.' I gave him the full glare, as you might imagine.

But I can't pretend everyone is either accommodating, or crestfallen. Pin-striped geezers, bolshie buggers, macho types with tittling women in tow: they can get tricky. I might run through one of my routines and they'd say, 'Who precisely do you think you are?' or, 'Oh, just bugger off, will you?' – things like that, not really addressing the issue, and some will give me a look as if *I'm* the weirdo and turn their backs. I don't like that sort of behaviour, I think it's discourteous, so I might give the arm that's holding the drink a little nudge, which helps turn them round towards me, and if they're by themselves I'll go up close and say, 'Know what, you're a *fucking cunt*, and I'll be keeping my eye on you.' They don't generally like being spoken to in this way. Of course, if there's a woman present I moderate my language. 'What's it like', I ask, then pause as if seeking the exact description, 'being an *utterly selfish berk?*'

One of them summoned a Festival Hall usher. I could see his plan, so I went and sat down with a modest glass of water, slipped off my heraldic badge and became horribly reasonable. 'So glad he's brought you over. I was looking for someone to ask. What exactly is the Hall's policy on persistent and unmuffled coughers? Presumably at some point you take steps to exclude them. If you could explain the complaints procedure, I'm sure many people in the audience tonight would happily support my proposal that you refuse all future bookings to this, er, gentleman.'

Andrew keeps on thinking up practical solutions. He says I should go to the Wigmore Hall instead. He says I should stay at home and listen to my records. He says I spend so much time being a vigilante that I can't possibly be concentrating on the music. I tell him I don't want to go to the Wigmore Hall: I'm saving chamber music for later. I want to go to the Festival Hall, the Albert Hall and the Barbican, and no one's going to stop me. Andrew says I should sit in the cheap seats, in the choir or among the Prommers. He says people who sit in expensive seats are like people – indeed, probably are the same people – who drive BMWs, Range Rovers and big Volvos, just fucking cunts, what do I expect?

I tell him I have two proposals to improve behaviour. The first would be the installation of overhead spotlights, and if someone made a noise above a certain level – one stated in the programme, but also printed on the ticket so that non-programme-buyers would also be alerted to the punishment – then the light over their seat would come on and the person would have to sit there, as if in the stocks, for the rest of the concert. My second suggestion would be more discreet. Every seat in the hall would be wired, and a small electric shock administered, whose strength would vary according to the volume of the occupant's cough, sniffle or sneeze. This would – as laboratory experiments on different species have shown – tend to discourage the offender from offending again.

Andrew said that apart from legal considerations, he foresaw two main objections to my plan. The first was that if you gave a human being an electric shock, he or she might very well react by making more noise than he or she had done in the first place, which would be somewhat counter-productive. And secondly, much as he wanted to encourage my scheme, he was minded to conclude that the practical effect of electrocuting concert-goers might well be to make them less willing to book tickets in future. Of course, if the London Philharmonic played to a completely empty hall, then he could see there wouldn't be any extraneous noises for me to worry about. So yes, that would achieve my aim, although without any bums on seats except my own, the orchestra might require an unrealistically high level of spon-sorship.

Andrew can be so provoking, don't you think? I asked him if he had ever tried listening to the still, sad music of humanity while someone was using a mobile phone.

'I wonder what instrument that would be played on,' he replied. 'Perhaps not an instrument at all. What you would do is strap a thousand or so concert-goers into their seats and quietly pass an electric current through them while telling them not to make a noise or they'll get an even bigger shock. You'd get muted groans and moans and assorted muffled squeaks – and that's the still, sad music of humanity.'

'You're such a cynic,' I said. 'Actually, that's not such a bad idea.'

'How old are you?'

'You ought to know. You forgot my last birthday.'

'That only shows how old I am. Go on, say the words.'

'Three years older than you.'

'Ergo?'

'Sixty-two.'

'And, correct me if I'm wrong, but you haven't always been like this?'

'No, doctor.'

'When you were a young man, you used to go to concerts and just sit there and listen happily to the music?'

'As far as I can remember, doctor.'

'And is it that others are now behaving worse, or that you are getting more sensitive with age?'

'People *are* behaving worse. That's what makes me more sensitive.'

'And when did you notice this change in people's behaviour?'

'When you stopped coming with me.'

'We don't talk about that.'

'I'm not. You asked the question. That's when they started behaving worse. When you stopped coming with me.'

Andrew thought about this for a while. 'Which proves my point. You only started noticing when you started going alone. So it's all about you, not them.'

'Then come with me again and it'll stop.'

'We don't talk about that.'

'No, we don't talk about that.'

A couple of days later I tripped up a man on the stairs. He had been especially offensive. Arriving at the last minute with a floozie in a short skirt; leaning back with his legs apart and looking around with needless turnings of the head; chatting and cuddling in the breaks between movements (the Sibelius concerto, of all things); programme-rustling, of course. And then, in the final movement, guess what he did? Leaned across to his companion and did some double-stopping on the inside of her thigh. She pretended to ignore it, then fondly batted at his hand with her programme, at which he sat back with a contented grin on his stupid, smug face.

At the interval I made straight for them. He was, shall we say, unacquiescent. Pushed past me with no more than a 'Fuck off, Charlie.' So I followed them, out and then across to those side-stairs at level 2A. He was clearly in a hurry. Probably wanted to hawk and spit and cough and sneeze and smoke and drink and set off his digital watch alarm to remind him to use his mobile phone. So I caught him on the ankle with a kick and he went down half a flight on his face. He was a heavy man, and there seemed to be blood. The woman he was with, who hadn't been any more civil, and had smirked when he said, 'Fuck off, Charlie,' began screaming. Yes, I thought, as I turned away, maybe in future you'll learn to treat the Sibelius violin concerto with more respect.

It's all about respect, isn't it? And if you don't have it, you have to be taught it. The true test, the only test, is whether we're becoming more civilized or whether we aren't. Wouldn't you agree?

# BARK

On the feast-day of Jean-Etienne Delacour, the following dishes had been prepared on the instructions of his daughter-in-law, Mme Amélie: bouillon, the beef which had been boiled in it, a grilled hare, a pigeon casserole, vegetables, cheese and fruit jellies. In a spirit of reluctant sociability, Delacour allowed a dish of bouillon to be placed before him; he even, in honour of the day, raised a ceremonial spoonful to his lips and blew graciously, before lowering it again untouched. When the beef was brought in, he nodded at the servant, who laid in front of him, on separate plates, a single pear and a slice of bark cut from a tree some twenty minutes earlier. Delacour's son Charles, daughter-in-law, grandson, nephew, nephew's wife, the curé, a neighbouring farmer, and Delacour's old friend André Lagrange, all made no observation. Delacour for his part civilly kept pace with those around him, eating one quarter of the pear while they consumed their beef, one quarter alongside the hare, and so on. When the cheese was brought in, he took out a pocket-knife and cut the tree bark into slices, then chewed each piece slowly to oblivion. Later, as aids to sleep, he took a cup of milk, some stewed lettuce and a rennet apple. His bedroom was well ventilated and his pillow stuffed with horsehair. He ensured that his chest was not weighed down with blankets, and that his feet would remain warm. As he settled his linen nightcap around his temples, Jean-Etienne reflected contentedly on the folly of those around him.

He was now sixty-one. In his earlier days, he had been both a gambler and a gourmand, a combination that had frequently threatened to inflict penury on his household.

Wherever dice were thrown or cards turned, wherever two or more beasts could be induced to race against one another for the gratification of spectators, Delacour was to be found. He had won and lost at faro and hazard, backgammon and dominoes, roulet and rouge et noir. He would play pitch-and-toss with an infant, bet his horse on a cockfight, play two-pack patience with Mme V—, and solitaire when he could find no rival or companion.

It was said that his gourmandism had put an end to his gambling. Certainly, there was not room in such a man for both these passions fully to express themselves. The moment of crisis had occurred when a goose reared to within days of slaughter – a goose he had fed with his own hand, and savoured in advance down to the last giblet – was lost in a trice at a hand of piquet. For a while, he sat between his two temptations like the proverbial ass between two bales of hay; but rather than starve to death like the indecisive beast, he acted as a true gambler, and let a toss of the coin decide the matter.

Thereafter, his stomach and his purse both swelled, while his nerves became calmer. He ate meals fit for a cardinal, as the Italians say. He would discourse on the point of esculence of every foodstuff, from capers to woodcock; he could explain how the shallot had been introduced into France by the returning Crusaders, and the cheese of Parma by Monsieur le Prince de Talleyrand. When a partridge was placed in front of him he would remove the legs, take a bite from each in a considered manner, nod judicially, and announce on which leg the partridge had been accustomed to rest its weight while sleeping. He was also a familiar of the bottle. If grapes were offered as a dessert, he would push them away with the words, 'I am not in the habit of taking my wine in the form of pills.'

Delacour's wife had approved his choice of vice, since

gourmandism is more likely to keep a man at home than gambling. The years passed, and her silhouette began to ape that of her husband. They lived plumply and easily until one day, fortifying herself in mid-afternoon while her husband was absent, Mme Delacour choked to death on a chicken bone. Jean-Etienne cursed himself for having left his wife unattended; he cursed his gourmandism, complicity in which had led to her death; and he cursed fate, chance, whatever governs our days, for having lodged the chicken bone at just such a murderous angle in her throat.

When his initial grief began to recede, he accepted lodging with Charles and Mme Amélie. He began a study of the law, and could often be found absorbed in the Nine Codes of the Kingdom. He knew the rural code by heart, and comforted himself with its certainties. He could cite the laws concerned with the swarming of bees and the making of compost; he knew the penalties for ringing church bells during a storm and for selling milk which had come into contact with copper pans; word for word, he recited ordinances governing the behaviour of wet-nurses, the pasturing of goats in forests, and the burial of dead animals found on the public highway.

For a while he continued with his gourmandizing, as if to do otherwise would be faithless to the memory of his wife; but though his stomach was still in it, his heart was not. What led to the abandonment of his former passion was a decision by the municipality in the autumn of 18— that, as a matter of hygiene and general beneficence, a public bathhouse should be built. That a man who had greeted the invention of a new dish as an astronomer would laud the discovery of a new star should be brought to temperance and moderation by a matter of soap and water moved some to mockery and others to moralizing. But Delacour had always given little heed to the opinions of others.

The death of his wife had brought a small legacy. Mme Amélie proposed that it might be both a prudent and a civic gesture for him to invest it in the building of the baths. The municipality, in order to excite interest, had devised a scheme based upon an Italian idea. The sum to be raised was divided into forty equal lots; each of the subscribers was obliged to be over forty years of age. Interest would be paid at the rate of two and a half per cent per annum, and upon the death of an investor the interest accruing to his share would be divided among the remaining subscribers. Simple mathematics led to a simple temptation: the last surviving investor would, from the thirty-ninth death until his own, enjoy an annual interest equal to the full sum of his original stake. The loans would terminate upon the death of the final subscriber, when the capital would be returned to the nominated heirs of the forty investors.

When Mme Amélie first mentioned the scheme to her husband, he was doubtful. 'You do not think, my dear, that it might awaken my father's old passion?'

'It can scarcely be called gambling when there is no possibility of losing.'

'That is surely what all gamblers constantly claim.'

Delacour approved his daughter-in-law's suggestion, and followed the progress of the subscription keenly. As each new investor came forward, he entered the man's name in a pocket-book, adding his date of birth and general remarks upon his health, appearance and genealogy. When a landowner fifteen years his senior joined the scheme, Delacour was merrier than at any time since the death of his wife. After a few weeks, the list was filled, whereupon he wrote to the other thirty-nine subscribers suggesting that since they had all, as it were, enlisted in the same regiment, they might choose to distinguish themselves by some sartorial mark, such as a ribbon in the coat. He also proposed that they institute a supper to be held annually for subscribers – he had almost written 'survivors'.

Few looked favourably on either proposal; some did not even reply; but Delacour continued to view his fellow subscribers as comrades-in-arms. If he met one in the street he would salute him warmly, enquire about his health, and exchange a few general words, perhaps about cholera. With his friend Lagrange, who had also subscribed, he would pass long hours at the Café Anglais, playing actuary with the lives of the other thirty-eight.

The municipal baths had not yet been declared open when the first investor died. Jean-Etienne, at supper with his family, proposed a toast to the over-optimistic and now lamented septuagenarian. Later, he took out his pocketbook and made an entry, with a date, then drew a long black line underneath.

Mme Amélie commented to her husband on the high spirits of her father-in-law, which seemed to her inappropriate.

'Death in general is his friend,' Charles replied. 'It is only his own death that should be considered his enemy.'

Mme Amélie briefly wondered if this was a philosophical truth or an empty platitude. She had an amiable nature, and worried little about her husband's actual opinions. She was more concerned about the manner in which he delivered them, which was increasingly beginning to resemble that of his father.

Along with a large engraved certificate of subscription, investors also received the right to use the baths gratis 'for the full period of investment'. Few were expected to do so, since those wealthy enough to subscribe were certainly wealthy enough to own a bathtub. But Delacour took to invoking his right first on a weekly, then on a daily basis. Some regarded this as an abuse of the municipality's benevolence, but Delacour was unswayed. His days now followed a fixed pattern. He would rise early, eat a single fruit, drink two glasses of water, and walk for three hours. Then he would visit the baths, where he soon became familiar with the attendants; as a subscriber, he was allowed a special towel reserved for his use. Afterwards, he would make his way to the Café Anglais, where he would discuss matters of the day with his friend Lagrange. Matters of the day, in Delacour's mind, rarely amounted to more than two: any foreseeable diminution of the subscribers' list, and the lax application of various laws by the municipality. Thus it had, in his opinion, insufficiently advertised the scale of reward for the destruction of wolves: 25 francs for a she-wolf in cub, 18 francs for a she-wolf not in cub, 12 for a male wolf, 6 for a cub, the amounts to be payable within a week following veri-fication of the evidence.

Lagrange, whose mind was of a contemplative rather than a theoretical cast, considered this complaint. 'And yet I do not know of anyone', he commented mildly, 'who has observed a wolf in the last eighteen months.'

'The more reason why the populace should be prompted to vigilance.'

Delacour next denounced the lack of stringency and frequency with which wine was tested for adulteration. By Article 38 of the law of 19th July 1791, still applicable, a fine of up to 1000 francs, and imprisonment for a period of up to one year, might be imposed upon those who mixed litharge, fish glue, extract of Campeche wood, or other noxious substances, with the wine they sold.

'You drink only water,' Lagrange pointed out. He raised his own glass and peered at the wine within. 'Besides, if our host were to embark on such practices, it might very happily reduce the list of subscribers.'

'I do not intend to win in such a fashion.'

Lagrange was disturbed by the harshness of his friend's

tone. 'Win,' he repeated. 'You can only win, if you call it winning, by my death.'

'That I shall regret,' said Delacour, evidently unable to conceive of an alternative outcome.

After the Café Anglais, Delacour would return home and read works on physiology and diet. Twenty minutes before supper he would cut himself a fresh slice of tree bark. While others ate their life-shortening concoctions, he would expatiate upon general threats to health and the lamentable impediments to human immortality.

These impediments gradually reduced the original list of forty subscribers. With each death, Delacour's good cheer increased, and so did the strictness of his regimen. Exercise, diet, sleep; regularity, temperance, study. One work of physiology indicated, with veiled phrasing and a sudden burst of Latin, that a reliable mark of health in the human male was the frequency with which he engaged in sexual connection. Both total abstinence and excessive indulgence were potentially harmful, although not as harmful as certain practices associated with abstinence. But a moderate frequency – for example, exactly once per week – was deemed to be salutary.

Delacour, convinced of this practical necessity, rendered up excuses to his dead wife, and entered into an arrangement with a maid at the baths, whom he visited once a week. She was grateful for the money he left, and once he had discouraged displays of affection, he looked forward to their exchange. He decided that when the thirty-ninth subscriber died, he would give her a hundred francs, or perhaps a little less, in recognition of her life-prolonging services.

More investors died; Delacour entered their terminal dates in his pocketbook and smilingly toasted their departures. On one such evening Mme Amélie, after retiring, said to her husband, 'What is the reason for living if it is only to outlive others?'

'Each of us must find his own reason,' Charles replied. 'That is his.'

'But do you not find it strange that what seems to afford him most joy nowadays is the death of his fellow men? He takes no customary pleasure in life. His days are ordered as if in obedience to the strictest duty – and yet, duty to what, duty to whom?'

'The subscription was your proposal, my dear.'

'I did not foresee, when I proposed it, the effect it might have upon his character.'

'My father's character', replied Charles sternly, 'is unchanged. He is an old man now, and a widower. Naturally his pleasures are diminished and his interests have altered somewhat. Yet he applies the same vigour of mind and the same logic to what interests him now as he did to what interested him before. His character has not changed,' Charles repeated, as if his father were being charged with senility.

André Lagrange, had he been asked, would have agreed with Mme Amélie. Once a voluptuary, Delacour had become an ascetic; once an advocate of toleration, Delacour had developed a severity towards other mortals. Seated at the Café Anglais, Lagrange listened to a peroration concerning the inadequate enforcement of the eighteen articles governing the cultivation of tobacco. Then there was a silence, a sip of water was taken, and Delacour continued, 'Every man should have three lives. This is my third.'

Bachelorhood, marriage, widowerhood, Lagrange supposed. Or perhaps gambling, gourmandism, the tontine. But Lagrange had been contemplative for long enough to recognize that men were often provoked to universal statement by some everyday event whose significance was being exaggerated.

'And her name?' he asked.

'It is strange', said Delacour, 'how, as life proceeds, the dominant sentiments may change. When I was young I respected the priest, I honoured my family, I was full of ambition. As for the passions of the heart, I discovered, when I met the woman who was to become my wife, how a long prologue of love leads finally, with the sanction and approval of society, to those carnal delights which we hold so dear. Now that I have grown older, I am less persuaded that the priest can show us the best way to God, my family often exasperates me, and I have no ambition left.'

'That is because you have acquired a certain wealth and a certain philosophy.'

'No, it is more that I judge mind and character rather than social rank. The curé is a pleasant companion but a theological fool; my son is honest but tedious. Observe that I do not claim virtue for this change in my understanding. It is merely something that has happened to me.'

'And carnal delight?'

Delacour sighed and shook his head. 'When I was a young man, in my army years, before meeting my late wife, I naturally accommodated myself with the sort of women who made themselves available. Nothing in those experiences of my youth advised me of the possibility that carnal delight might lead to feelings of love. I imagined – no, I was sure – that it was always the other way round.'

'And her name?'

'The swarming of bees,' replied Delacour. 'As you know, the law is clear. So long as the owner follows his bees as they swarm, he has the right to reclaim and take possession of them again. But if he has failed to follow them, then the proprietor of the ground on which they alight has legal title to them. Or, take the case of rabbits. Those rabbits which pass from one warren to another become the property of the man on whose land the second warren is situated, unless this proprietor has enticed them thither by means of fraud or artifice. As with pigeons and doves. If they fly to common land, they belong to whomsoever may kill them. If they fly to another dovecote, they belong to the owner of that dovecote, provided again that he has not enticed them thither by fraud or artifice.'

'You have quite lost me.' Lagrange looked on benignly, familiar with such perambulations from his friend.

'I mean that we make such certainties as we can. But who can foresee when the bees might swarm? Who can foresee whither the dove might fly, or when the rabbit might tire of its warren?'

'And her name?'

'Jeanne. She is a maid at the baths.'

'Jeanne who is a maid at the baths?' Everyone knew Lagrange for a mild man. Now he stood up quickly, kicking his chair backwards. The noise reminded Delacour of his army days, of sudden challenges and broken furniture.

'You know her?'

'Jeanne who is a maid at the baths? Yes. And you must renounce her.'

Delacour did not understand. That is to say, he understood the words but not their motive or purpose. 'Who can foresee whither the dove might fly?' he repeated, pleased with this formulation.

Lagrange was leaning over him, knuckles on the table, almost trembling, it seemed. Delacour had never seen his friend so serious, or so angry. 'In the name of our friendship you must renounce her,' he repeated.

'You have not been listening.' Delacour leaned back in his chair, away from his friend's face. 'At the start it was simply a matter of hygiene. I insisted on the girl's docility. I wanted no caresses in return – I discouraged them. I paid her little attention. And yet, in spite of all this, I have come to love her. Who can foresee –'

'I have been listening, and in the name of our friendship, I insist.'

Delacour considered the request. No, it was a demand, not a request. He was suddenly back at the card table, faced by an opponent who for no evident reason had raised his bid tenfold. At such moments, assessing the inexpressive fan in his opponent's hands, Delacour had always relied on instinct, not calculation.

'No,' he replied quietly, as if laying down a small trump.

Lagrange left.

Delacour sipped his glass of water and calmly reviewed the possibilities. He reduced them to two: disapproval or jealousy. He ruled out disapproval: Lagrange had always been an observer of human behaviour, not a moralist who condemned its vagaries. So it must be jealousy. Of the girl herself, or of what she represented and proved: health, longevity, victory? Truly, the subscription was driving men to strange behaviour. It had made Lagrange over-excited, and he had gone off like a swarm of bees. Well, Delacour would not follow him. Let him land wherever he chose.

Delacour continued with his daily routine. He did not mention Lagrange's defection to anyone, and constantly expected him to reappear at the café. He missed their discussions, or at least Lagrange's attentive presence; but gradually he resigned himself to the loss. He began to visit Jeanne more frequently. She did not question this, and listened as he talked of legal matters she rarely understood. Having previously been warned against impertinent expressions of affection, she remained quiet and tractable, while not failing to notice that his caresses had become gentler. One day she informed him that she was with child.

'Twenty-five francs,' he replied automatically. She

protested that she was not asking for money. He apologized – his mind had been elsewhere – and asked if she was confident the child was his. On hearing her assurance – or, more exactly, the tone of her assurance, which had none of the vehemence of mendacity – he offered to have the baby placed with a wet-nurse and to provide an allowance for it. He kept to himself the surprising love he had come to feel for Jeanne. To his mind, it was not really her affair; it concerned him, not her, and he also felt that were he to express what he felt, it might depart, or become complicated in a way that he did not desire. He let her understand that she could rely upon him; that was enough. Otherwise, he enjoyed his love as a private matter. It had been a mistake telling Lagrange; doubtless it would be a mistake telling anyone else.

A few months later, Lagrange became the thirty-sixth member of the tontine to die. Since Delacour had told no one of their quarrel, he felt obliged to attend the funeral. As the coffin was being lowered, he remarked to Mme Amélie, 'He did not sufficiently take care of himself.' When he looked up he saw, standing at the back of a group of mourners on the other side of the grave, Jeanne, her dress now full in front of her.

The law relating to wet-nurses was in his view ineffective. The declaration of 29th January 1715 was plain enough. Wet-nurses were forbidden from suckling two infants at the same time, on pain of correctional punishment for the woman and a fine of 50 francs for her husband; they were obliged to declare their own pregnancies as soon as the second month was reached; they were also forbidden to send back infants to the parental home, even in cases of non-payment, but were obliged to continue their service and be reimbursed later by the police tribunal. Yet everyone knew that such women could not always be trusted. They made arrangements with other infants; they lied about the advancement of their pregnancies; and if there was a dispute over payment between parents and wet-nurse, the child would often not survive the following week. Perhaps he should permit Jeanne to feed the child herself after all, since that was what she wanted.

At their next encounter, Delacour expressed surprise at her presence by the graveside. Lagrange had never, as far as he knew, exercised the right to use the municipal baths.

'He was my father,' she replied.

Of Paternity and Filiation, he thought. Decree of 23rd March 1803, promulgated 2nd April. Chapters One, Two and Three.

'How?' was all he could say.

'How?' she repeated.

'Yes, how?'

'In the usual manner, I am sure,' replied the girl.

'Yes.'

'He used to visit my mother as . . .'

'As I visit you.'

'Yes. He was much taken with me. He wished to acknowledge me, to make me . . .'

'Legitimate?'

'Yes. My mother did not want this. There was a dispute. She feared he would try to steal me. She guarded me. Sometimes he would spy on us. When she was dying, my mother made me promise never to receive him or to have contact with him. I promised. I did not think that . . . that the funeral amounted to contact.'

Jean-Etienne Delacour sat on the girl's narrow bed. Something was slipping in his mind. The world was making less sense than it should. This child, provided it survived the hazards of accouchement, would be Lagrange's grandchild. What he chose not to tell me, what Jeanne's mother kept from him, what I in my turn have not told Jeanne. We make the laws but the bees swarm anyway, the rabbit seeks a different warren, the pigeon flies to another's dovecote.

'When I was a gambler,' he said finally, 'people disapproved. They judged it a vice. I never thought so. To me it seemed the application of logical scrutiny to human behaviour. When I was a gourmand, people judged it an indulgence. I never thought so. To me it seemed a rational approach to human pleasure.'

He looked at her. She seemed to have no idea what he was talking about. Well, that was his own fault. 'Jeanne,' he said, taking her hand, 'you need have no fear for your child. No fear of the kind your mother had. It is not necessary.'

'Yes, sir.'

At supper he listened to his grown-up son's prattle and declined to correct numerous idiocies. He chewed on a sliver of tree bark, but without appetite. Later, his cup of milk tasted as if it had come from a copper pan, his stewed lettuce stank of the dunghill, his rennet apple had the texture of a horsehair pillow. In the morning, when they found him, his linen nightcap was grasped in a rigid hand, though whether he had been about to put it on, or whether for some reason he had just chosen to remove it, no one could tell.

# Knowing French

Dear Dr Barnes, (Me, old woman, rising eighty-one),

Well, so I read serious WORKS, but for light reading in the evenings, what does one do for fiction in an Old Folkery? (You will understand that I have not been here long.) Plenty enough 'Fiction' provided by the Red Cross. What about? Why! the doctor with the crinkled hair 'greying at the temples', probably misunderstood by his wife, or better still a widower, and the attractive nurse who hands him the saw in the theatre. Even at an age when I might have been susceptible to such an implausible view of life, I preferred Darwin's 'Vegetable Mould and Earthworms'.

So: I thought, why not go to the public library and go through all the fiction beginning with A? (A little girl once asked me: 'I understand about the Stag Brewery but what's the Lie Brewery?') Thus I find I have read many entertaining descriptions of pubs, and much voyeurism on women's breasts, so I pass on. You see where I am going? The next lot I come to is Barnes: 'Flaubert's Parrot'. Ah, that must be Loulou. I flatter myself that I know 'Un Coeur simple' by heart. But I have few books as my room here is trop petite.

You will be glad to know that I am bilingual and pronounce a treat. Last week in the street I heard a schoolmaster say to a tourist, 'A gauche puis à droite.' The subtlety of the pronunciation of GAUCHE made my day, and I keep saying it to myself in the bath. As good as French bread-and-butter. Would you believe that my father, who would now be 130, was taught French (as Latin then was) pronounced as English: 'lee tchatt'. No, you wouldn't: not sure myself. But there has been some progress: the R is frequently rolled in the right direction nowadays by students.

But revenons à nos perroquets, which is my main reason for writing. I am not taking you up on what you say in your book about coincidence. Well, yes I am. You say that you do not believe in coincidence. You cannot mean this. You mean that you do not believe in intentional or purposeful coincidence. You cannot deny the existence of coincidence, since it happens with some frequency. You refuse, however, to attribute any significance to it. I am less certain than you, being on the whole agnostic in such matters. Anyway, I am in the habit, most mornings, of walking down Church Street (no church remaining) towards Market Green (no market either). Yesterday I had just laid down your book and was walking along, when what do I see, caged behind a high window, but a large grey parrot in its cage? Coincidence? Of course. Meaning? The beast looks miserable, feathers all fluffed up, coughing, a drip from its beak, and no toys in its cage. So I write a (polite) postcard to its (unknown) owner saying that this situation wrings my heart, and I hope when they get back in the evenings they are kind to the bird. Hardly am I back in my room when a furious old woman storms in, introduces herself, brandishes my postcard and says she will take me to court. 'Good,' I reply. 'You will find it very expensive.' She tells me that 'Dominic' fluffs up his feathers because he is a show-off. He has no toys in his cage because he is not a budgerigar and wd. destroy them if he had. And that parrots' beaks cannot drip because they have no mucous membrane. 'You are an ignorant, interfering old woman,' she flings at me as she marches away.

Now, this dissertation on parrots has impressed me. Mrs Audrey Penn is an educated woman, clearly. Having no other reference book to hand but my old college register, I idly look her up. There she is: Lady Margaret Hall, eight years junior to me, exhibitioner where I was top scholar, and reading <u>French</u>. (Not veterinary science.)

I had to write this to you as nobody else would understand the oddity of the synchronicity. But whether all this constitutes a coincidence in the fullest sense, I am not equipped to say. My fellow incarcerees here are either mad or deaf. I, like Félicité, am deaf. Unfortunately the mad ones are not deaf, but who am I to say that the deaf ones are not mad? In fact, though the youngest, I am Head Girl, because, through comparative youth, I am comparatively competent.

Croyez, cher Monsieur, à l'assurance de mes sentiments distingués.
Sylvia Winstanley

4 March 1986

Dear Mr Barnes,

So why did you say you were a doctor? As for me, I am a spinster, though you are ungenerous to offer me the choice of only Miss, Mrs or Ms. Why not Lady Sylvia? I am Upper Clarce after all, 'senior county family' and all that. My great aunt told me that when she was a little girl Cardinal Newman brought her an orange back from Spain. One for her and one for each of her sisters. The fruit was then unfamiliar in England. N. was grandmother's godfather.

The warden tells me that Dominic's owner is 'well thought of in the district', so obviously gossip is going the rounds and I had better keep my mouth shut. I wrote a conciliatory letter (no reply), and noticed when next I passed by that Dominic had been taken out of the window. Perhaps he is sick. After all, if parrots have no mucous membrane, why was his beak dripping? But if I go on asking such questions publicly, I shall have my day in court. Well, I am not afeared of the magistrates.

I have taught a lot of Gide. Proust bores me, and I do not understand Giraudoux, having a funny kind of brain that is brilliant in some areas and bone-stupid in others. I was supposed to be a dead cert for a First, the Principal said she would eat her hat if I didn't get one. I didn't (II, with Distinction in Spoken Language) and she took it up with the authorities; answer came that the number of Alphas was balanced by the number of Gammas; no Betas at all. See what I mean? I didn't go to propah school, and being a 'lady' didn't learn orthodox subjects, so at the Entrance Examination my essay on the maternal habits of the earwig did me more good than the 'educated' ones of the girls from Sherborne. I was a top scholar as I think I told you.

Now why did you say you were a doctor in your sixties when you obviously can't be more than forty? Come, now! In youth I discovered that men were deceivers ever, and decided not to take up Flirting until I came onto the Old Age Pension at 60 – but this has led me to a further 20 years of being – my psychologist tells me – an outrageous flirt.

Having done Barnes, I move on to Brookner, Anita, and blessed if she didn't appear on the Box that very day. I don't know, I don't know. THEY are certainly doing things to me. E.G. I say, 'If that is a right decision, let me see a stag,' choosing the most unlikely creature for that place. Stag appears. Ditto kingfisher and spotted woodpecker on other occasions. I can't accept that this is imagination, or that my subconscious was aware that these creatures were lurking in the wings. There would seem to be as it were a High Self that, for instance, tells an ignorant red cell to go and make a clot over a knife-cut. But then what is in charge of your high self and my high self teaching our blood to go and mend the cuts? On 'Hospital Watch' I noticed that they just rammed all the raw meat back into the hole and left it to remake itself into muscles on its own, and I had a very major operation three months ago, but all the bits seem to have come together in the right shape and done the right thing. Who showed them how?

Have I room on page for some parrot feathers? The Principal, Miss Thurston, was a rather graceless, horse-faced woman, 24 years my senior, 'assoiffée de beauté', and wore unsuitable picture hats in which she bicycled (Cambridge-style, basket behind). At one time we were very close, and planned to share a house, but she discovered, just in time, how nasty I am. One night I dreamed of Miss Thurston: she was dancing with joy; she had on an enormous hat with parrot feathers flying from it. She said, 'All is now well between us' (or something of the sort). I said to myself, 'But this woman was never PLAIN.' At breakfast I told my cousin, 'I am sure Miss Thurston is dead.' We look in the Telegraph – no obituary, as there would have been. The post comes – on back of envelope, 'As-tu vu que Miss Thurston est morte?' We visit other cousin; obituary and photograph in the Times newspaper. I have to add that I am not in the least 'psychic'.

I won't say I didn't mean to preach as I did. I am Head Girl here as the YOUNGEST and the most competent. Have car, can drive. As most of them are stone-deaf, there is little whispering in corners. Can I make a grand word for immense letter-writing (epistolomania?). I do apologize.

Best wishes, good fortune with your writing,
Sylvia Winstanley

18 April 1986

Dear Julian,

I call you so with permission, and having been granted leave to Flirt; although Flirting with only a dust-jacket to go on is a new experience as you may imagine. As for why I chose to incarcerate myself in an Old Folkery when I can walk and drive and be cheered by the threat of law courts, it was a matter of jumping before pushed, or sauter pour mieux reculer. My dear cousin died, I was threatened with a major operation, and found the prospect of being Housekeeper to Myself until I conked out unappealing. And then there was, as they put it, an Unexpected Vacancy. I am a Maverick as you may have deduced and find the common wisdom just that. The C. W. states that we are all expected to remain independent for as long as possible and then succumb to an Old Folkery when our family can no longer endure us or we start leaving gas-taps on and scalding ourselves with our Ovaltine. But in these circs the O. F. is likely to come as a severe jolt, causing us to lose our marbles, mutate into cabbages, giving swift rise to another Unexpected Vacancy. So I resolved to transport myself here while still largely functioning. Well, I have no children and my psychologist agreed.

Now, dear Barnes, alas! The only book of yours you told me not to read was the only one available at the library. 'Before She Met Me' has been taken out 11 times since January, you will be fascinated to know, and one reader has heavily scored through the word 'fuck' whenever it occurs. However, he has condescended to read it all the way to the last 'fuck' on p. 178. I have not got so far yet. I tried a spot of raconterie at supper to the other deafs, but without success. 'I suppose,' I said, 'this book is about the Pleasures of the Bed.' 'Wot? Wot? Poddon? Poddon?' 'Plezzers! You know! nice comfy pillow, soft mattress, sleepy-byes.' So nobody thought this raconte-worthy. Well, I shall read it and no doubt learn a lot.

I am very cross, sore, etc., owing to excessive barrack-room rudeness from Warden's husband, ex-sergeant-major, whom I would fain have pushed backwards downstairs, but realized he was likely to be stronger. Let me preach some more to you, this time on the subject of Old Folkeries. When Nanny finally started going gaga, I investigated a number of such établissements. It does not raise the spirits to see, time after time, the same crescent of obedient biddies sitting in cheap armchairs while the Box blares at them like Mussolini. At one place I said to the Warden, 'What sort of activities do you provide?' She looked at me incredulously, for wasn't it clear the old deafs were already having as thrilling a time as mind and spirit could bear? Eventually she replied, 'They have a man who comes for games once a week.' 'Games?' I asked, seeing not many takers for the Olympics. 'Yes', she replied condescendingly. 'He gets them into a circle and throws a beach-ball at them and they have to throw it back.' Well: I made a remark about beach-balls to the Sgt-Major this morning but not surprisingly it was lost on him. The deafs and the mads here are constantly afraid of Being a Nuisance. The only way of making sure you are not Being a Nuisance is to be in your coffin, so I intend to go on Being a Nuisance as a way of keeping alive. Whether I shall succeed or not, I don't know. This Old Folkery is working out exactly like something from Balzac. We disburse our lifetime's savings in order to hand over control of our lives. I imagined a system of enlightened dictatorship as approved by Voltaire, but wonder if such a government has or could ever exist. The wardens, whether by design or unconscious habit, are gradually eroding more and more of our spirits. The governing body are supposed to be our allies.

I was half-heartedly collecting 'sottises' for you; the one that annoys me most is the notion that in England we have something called 'the Summer' and that sooner or later 'it comes'. And then we all sit out in the garden after dinner being bitten by gnats. Granted 'tis about 10 degrees warmer and you can go out after tea. The middle-aged all tell me that when they were young summers were red-hot and you wassailed on hay-wains etc. but I tell them that as I am quite 30 years older I remember perfectly well that May was a lousy month in their youth, and they have forgotten all that. Have you come across 'Les trois saints de glace' – I forget who they are, but they have to be past before you can have a proper – Latin – summer. I spent one May in the Dordogne and it rained all the time and they were beastly to the dog and showed me their operations and bread was only made once a fortnight so sucks to Aquitaine! I love the Drôme, though.

Book I haven't read:     All Dickens
                         All Scott
                         All Thackeray
                         All Shakespeare except 'Macbeth'
                         All J Austen but one

I do hope you find a lovely gîte; I adore the Pyrenees; the flowers; and the little 'gaves'.

You see, I went round the world in 1935, before everything was spoilt. Also in a lot of boats, not <u>avions</u>.

You say, re coincidence, why not ask to see an armadillo or a snowy owl, that would test the power of intentional coincidence. I shall not rise to this, but will tell you that we lived in Putney back in XVI. Putney is next to Barnes.

Well, thanks a lot for writing. Now I'm feeling better, & the moon has come round the corner behind the pines.

Sylvia W.
Parrot D. back in window.

16 September 1986

Dear Julian,
Your novel has proved educational, not on sex lines, but because your character, Barbara, has exactly the same slippery methods of discussion as our Warden here. Her husband is the acme of insolence to me, yet I know that if the word 'bloody' slips out I am totally sunk with the Gov. Bod., which approves of me so far. Yesterday I was on the way to the letter-box when the Sgt-Major accosted me and suggested it was an unnecessary journey. All the deafs and mads here give him their letters to post for them. I said, 'I may no longer be driving my car but I shall continue taking the bus into town and am well capable of tottering to the letter-box.' He looked at me impertinently and I imagined him steaming open all the letters at night and tearing up any which contained complaints about the Old Folkery. If my letters suddenly cease you may conclude that either I am dead or else under the full control of the Authorities.

Are you musical? Well, I suppose I am a bit, but, only because being clever and starting the piano at age six, I very soon got good at sight-reading, playing also the double bass & flute (more or less) so constantly asked to play church organs. Liked making terrific roarings on these instruments. (Not church myself. Think own thoughts.) I like going into town – always badinage in the bus or morris dancing in the shopping precincts with Brandenburg Concertos on a machine and proper persons playing violins with them.

I have read some more As and Bs. One of these days I shall tot up the number of drinks consumed or cigarettes lit, for padding purposes in novels. Also 'vignettes' of waiters, taxi-drivers, vendeuses and others, who play no further part in the story. Novelists either go in for padding or else for philosophizing, what we were told to regard as 'generalizations', chez Balzac. Whom is the Novel for, I ask myself. In my own case for someone of an undemanding nature who requires to lose herself between about 10 p.m. and bedtime. This may be unsatisfac, for you, I can see. Also, to be able to do this, it is essential that there be a character sufficiently like myself to identify with and, Maverick that I am, there isn't often.

Still, the As and Bs remain a cut above the monthly supply from the Red Cross. They seem to be written by Night Nurses in the long hours when they have nothing else to do. And the sole theme is desire for marriage. What happens after marriage doesn't seem to have struck them, though to me that is really the crux.

A Famous Person in the art world wrote in his autobiography a few years ago that he first grew to love women by falling in love with a little girl at his prep school dance. He was eleven at the time, and she was nine. There is no doubt at all that I was that little girl: he describes my dress, and it was my brother's prep school, dates right, etc. Nobody else has fallen for me since, but I was a pretty child. If I had deigned to look at him, he says, he would have followed me to the end of his days. Instead he chased after women all his life and made his wife so unhappy that she became an alcoholic, whereas I never married. What do you deduce from this, Mr Novelist Barnes? Was this a missed opportunity seventy years ago? Or was it a fortunate escape on both our parts? Little did he know that I was to become a bluestocking and not at all up his street. Perhaps he would have driven me to drink and I would have driven him to philandering, nobody would have been better off except the wife he thereby wouldn't have had, and in his autobiography he would have said that he wished he'd never set eyes upon me. You are too young for this kind of question, but it is the sort you increasingly ask yourself as you become deaf and mad. Where would I be now if two years before the Great War I had glanced in a different direction?

Well, thank you enormously, and I hope your own life is satisfac. and offspring all you wd. wish.

With love from Sylvia W.

24 January 1987

Dear Julian,

One of the mads here has been seeing ghosts. They show themselves as little green flashes, in case you should wish to spot one, and they followed her here when she gave up her flat. Trouble is, whereas they were benign in their previous location, they have reacted to finding themselves incarcerated in an Old Folkery by playing the merry devil. We are each of us allowed a small refrigerator in our 'cubicles' in case of Night Starvation, and Mrs Galloway fills hers with chocolates and bottles of sweet sherry. So, what have the sprites been up to in the middle of the night but eating her chocolates and drinking her sherry! We all demonstrated due concern when this was raised – the deaf showing more concern, no doubt because they were unable to comprehend – and tried to offer condolences for her loss. This went on for a while, long faces being in order, until one day she came into Lunch looking like the Cheshire Cat. 'I got my own back!' she cried. 'I drank one of <u>their</u> bottles of sherry which they left in the fridge!' So we all celebrated. Alas, prematurely, for the chocolate continued to suffer nocturnal depredation, despite handwritten notes, both stern and pleading, which Mrs G took to leaving attached to the refrigerator door. (What languages do you think ghosts can read?) The matter finally went to the full assembly of Pilcher House one suppertime, with Warden and Sgt-Major present. How to prevent the spirits from eating her chocolate? All looked to Head Girl, who miserably failed the test. And for once I have to praise the Sgt-Major, who showed an estimable sense of irony, unless – which is perhaps more likely – he actually believes in the existence of the little green flashes. 'Why not get a fridge lock?' he suggested. Unanimous applause from Ds and Ms, where-upon he offers to go himself to B&Q to obtain one for her. I shall keep you au courant, in case this is useful for one of your books. Do you swear as much as your characters, I should like to know? Nobody swears here, except me, still internally.

Did you know my great friend Daphne Charteris? Maybe your great-aunt's sister-in-law? No, you said you were Middle Clarce in origin. She was one of our first aviatrices, Upper Clarce, daughter of a Scottish laird, used to ferry Dexter cattle around after she got her licence. One of only 11 women trained to fly a Lancaster in the war. Bred pigs and always named the runt of the litter Henry after her youngest brother. Had a room in her house known as the 'Kremlin' where even her husband wasn't allowed to disturb her. I always thought that was the secret of a happy marriage. Anyway, husband died and she went back to the family house to live with the runt Henry. The place was a pigsty, but they lived quite contentedly, getting deafer together by the month. When they could no longer hear the doorbell, Henry rigged up a car horn as a replacement. Daphne always refused to wear hearing aids on the grounds that they caught in the branches of trees.

In the middle of the night, while the ghosties are trying to pick Mrs Galloway's refrigerator lock to get at her Creme Eggs, I lie awake and watch the moon slowly move between the pines and think of the advantages of dying. Not that we are given a choice. Well, yes, there is self-slaughter, but that has always struck me as vulgar and self-important, like people who walk out of the theatre or the symphony concert. What I mean is – well, you know what I mean.

Main reasons for dying: it's what others expect when you reach my age; impending decrepitude and senility; waste of money – using up inheritance – keeping together brain-dead incontinent bag of old bones; decreased interest in The News, famines, wars, etc.; fear of falling under total power of Sgt-Major; desire to Find Out about Afterwards (or not?).

Main reasons for not dying: have never done what others expect, so why start now; possible distress caused to others (but if so, inevitable at any time); still only on B at Lie Brewery; who would infuriate Sgt-Major if not me?

– then I run out. Can you suggest others? I find that For always comes out stronger than Against.

Last week one of the mads was discovered stark naked at the bottom of the garden, suitcase filled with newspapers, apparently waiting for the train. No trains anywhere near the Old Folkery, needless to say, since Beeching got rid of the branch lines.

Well, thank you again for writing. Forgive epistolomania.
Sylvia

P.S. Why did I tell you that? What I was trying to say about Daphne is that she was always someone who looked forward, almost never back. This probably seems not much of a feat to you, but I promise it gets harder.

5 October 1987

Dear Julian,

Wouldn't you think language was for the purpose of communication? I was not allowed to teach at my first practice school (training college), only to listen to classes, as I got the tu of the Passé Simple wrong. Now if ever I had been taught Grammer, as opposed to Knowing French, I could have retorted that nobody would ever say 'Lui écrivis-tu?' or whatever. At my 'school' we were mainly taught phrases without analysis of tenses involved. I have constant letters from a Frenchwoman with an ordinary secondary education who happily writes 'J'était' or 'Elle s'est blessait' regardless. Yet my boss, who dismissed me, pronounced her French R's with that horrid muted sound used in English. I am glad to say all that is much improved and we no longer rhyme 'Paris' with 'Marry'.

I am not sure as yet whether the long letters I write have lapsed into senile garrulity. The point, Mr Novelist Barnes, is that Knowing French is different from Grammer, and that this applies to all aspects of life. I cannot find the letter in which you told me about meeting a writer even more antique than me (Gerrady? sp? – I looked for him in the library but could not find; in any case I shall surely have conked out before getting to the Gs). As I recall, he asked if you believed

in survival after death and you answered No and he replied,
'When you get to my age, you might.' I am not saying there
is life after death, but I am certain of one thing, that when
you are thirty or forty you may be very good at Grammer,
but by the time you get to be deaf or mad you also need to
know French. (Do you grasp what I mean?)

Oh! oh! oh! for a real croissant! Yet French bread is made
with French flour. Do they get that in your part of the world?
Last night we had corned beef hash and baked beans; I wish
I didn't love my food so. Sometimes I dream of apricots.
You cannot buy an apricot in this country, they all taste of
cotton wool impregnated with Austerity orange juice. After
<u>frateful</u> scene with Sgt-Major I cut lunch and had a samwidge
and knickerbocker glory in town.

You write that you are not afraid of dying as long as you
don't end up dead as a result. That sounds casuistical to me.
Anyway, perhaps you won't notice the transition. My friend
Daphne Charteris took a long time a-dying. 'Am I dead yet?'
she used to ask, and sometimes, 'How long have I been dead
for?' Her final words of all were, 'I've been dead for a while
now. Doesn't feel any different.'

There's nobody here to talk to about death. Morbid, you
see, and not <u>naice</u>. They don't mind talking about ghosties
and poltergeists and suchlike, but whenever I get going on
the real subject the Warden & Sgt-Major tell me I mustn't
scare the ducks. All part of my battle against the tabooing
of death as a subject – or Fear of It – and the energy with
which the medical profession tries to stop the dying from
dying, keeps alive babies born brainless, & enables barren
women to have artificial children. 'We have been trying for
a baby for six years' – Well! so you go without. The other
evening we all got double-yolked eggs – 'Why? This is
strange.' 'They are giving the pullets fertility drugs to bring
them into lay earlier.'

What do I keep in my refrigerator, you ask? My purse, if you must know, my address book, my correspondence, and a copy of my will. (Fire.)

Family still united? Yours? Any more children? I see you are doing your Modern Father stuff well. George V used to bath his children, Q. Mary didn't.

V. best wishes, and succès fou to you,
Sylvia

14 October 1987

Merci, charmant Monsieur, for the food parcel. Alas, the combination of the GPO & the Sgt-Major meant that the croissants were not as fresh as when they left you. I insisted on having a General Distribution of this Lease Lend, so all the deafs and mads got half each. 'Poddon? Poddon? Wozzit? Wozzit?' They prefer floppy triangles of white bread toast with Golden Shred. If I pushed the leftovers through the letter-box for Dominic – still in window – do you think Warden wd have me gated? Sorry only postcard, arm not good. Best wishes, Sylvia

10 December 1987

Barnes comes at about chest level, Brookner you have to get on the floor. I do think her 'Look At Me' is a beautiful piece of tragic writing, unlike 'King Lear' which I have just read for the 1st time. Apart from some purple patches, plot and characterization total balderdash. Emperor's clothes paradigm (word I've just learnt from crossword). Only postcard – Arm. V. best wishes, Sylvia

14 January 1989

Dear Julian,

(Yes! Old Winstanley), Please forgive more senile garrulity. Also state of handwriting, which wd shame Nanny.

Fascinating telly of lion-cubs trying to eat porc-épic (why épic? – Larousse says corruption of porcospino which is obvious but why not épine instead of épic?). I am not really attracted to the hedgehog – I had a cattle grid at my cottage into which hedgehogs constantly fell. I found lifting them out by hand was the simplest way, but they are vermin-ridden and have inexpressive eyes, rather mean.

Foolish and senile of me to go on about your children when you say you have none. Plse forgive. Of course you make things up in your stories.

As I am eighty-four and still have an excellent memory I know it is inevitable that coincidences should occur, e.g. parrots, French scholars, etc. But then the Famous Art Person. And a month ago, I learned that my great-niece Hortense Barret is to go to university to read agricultural science. (We had Forestry in our day. Did you have Foresters? Earnest young men with leather patches on their elbows who lived in colonies near Parks Road and went off together for Field Work?) So the same week I am reading a book about hydrangeas and learn that the Hortensia may have been named after a young woman called Hortense Barret who went on the Bougainville expedition with the botanist Commerson. Enquiries reveal that there were however many generations between them, in and out of marriage, names changing, but the line was direct. What do you make of that? And why had I chosen to read a book about hydrangeas? I own neither pot-plant nor window-box nowadays. So you see, one can't attribute all this to Great Age and Good Memory. It is as if a Mind from outside – not my own unconscious mind – were saying, 'Take note of this: we have our eyes upon you.' I am agnostic, I may say, though could accept the hypothesis of a 'guide' or 'surveillant', even a Guardian Angel.

If so, what about it? I am only telling you that I get this impression of a constant dig-in-the-ribs. 'Watch it!' and this I find of signal use to me. May not be your pigeon at all. To me it provides evidence of educational intent from Higher Mind. How is it done? Search me!

As I am on the psychic belt I notice how evolution in the understanding of the Mind is progressing almost at the speed of technology: ectoplasm as much dated as rushlights.

Mrs Galloway – she of the fridge lock and the green sprites – 'passed on' as the Warden likes to say. Everything passes here. Pass the marmalade, she passed such a remark, Did it Pass? they ask one another of their troublesome bowel movements. What do you think will happen to the little green flashes, I asked one dinner-time. Ds & Ms considered topic and eventually concluded that they probably passed on too.

Amitiés, sentiments distingués, etc.,
Sylvia W.

17 January 1989

I suppose, if you are Mad, and you die, & there is an Explanation waiting, they have to make you unmad first before you can understand it. Or do you think being Mad is just another veil of consciousness around our present world which has nothing to do with any other one?

Do not conclude from Cathedral postcard that I have stopped Thinking own Thoughts. 'Vegetable Mould and Earthworms' in all probability. But perhaps not.

S.W.

19 January 1989

So Mr Novelist Barnes,

If I asked you 'What is life?', you would probably reply, in so many words, that it is all just a coincidence.

So, the question remains, What sort of coincidence?

S.W.

3rd April 1989

Dear Mr Barnes,

Thank you for your letter of 22nd March. I regret to inform you that Miss Winstanley passed on two months ago. She fell and broke her hip on the way to the post-box, and despite the best efforts of the hospital, complications set in.

She was a lovely lady, and certainly the life and soul of the party around Pilcher House. She will be long remembered and much missed.

If you require any further information, please do not hesitate to contact me.

Yours faithfully,
J. Smyles (Warden)


10th April 1989

Dear Mr Barnes,

Thank you for your letter of the 5th inst.

In clearing out Miss Winstanley's room, we found a number of items of value in the refrigerator. There was also a small packet of letters but because they had been placed in the freezing compartment and then the fridge had been unfortunately switched off for defrosting they had suffered much damage. Although the printed letterhead was still legible we thought it might be distressing to the person to receive them back in this condition so regrettably we disposed of them. Perhaps this is what you were referring to.

We still miss Miss Winstanley very much. She was a lovely lady, and certainly the life and soul of the party around Pilcher House during her time here.

Yours faithfully,
J. Smyles (Warden)

# APPETITE

He has his good days. Of course, he has his bad days, too, but let's not think about them for the moment.

On his good days, I read to him. I read from one of his favourites: *The Joy of Cooking*, *The Constance Spry Recipe Book*, *Margaret Costa's Four Seasons Cookery*. They may not always work, but they're the most reliable, and I've learnt what he prefers and what to avoid. Elizabeth David's no use, and he hates the modern celebrity chefs. 'Ponces,' he shouts: 'Ponces with quiffs!' He doesn't like TV cooks either. 'Look at those cheap clowns,' he'll say, even though I'm just reading to him.

I once tried *Bon Viveur's London* 1954 on him, and was that a mistake. The doctors warned me that over-excitement was bad for him. But that's not much to tell me, is it? All the wisdom they've given me over the last years can be boiled down to this: we don't really know what causes it, we don't know how best to treat it, he'll have his good days and his bad days, don't over-excite him. Oh yes, and it is of course incurable.

He'll sit in his chair, in his pyjamas, with his dressing-gown on, shaved as well as I can do him, and with his feet tucked fully into his slippers. He isn't one of those men who wear down the backs of their slippers and turn them into espadrilles. He's always been very proper. So he sits with his feet together, heels in his slippers, waiting for me to open the book. I used to do this at random, but it caused problems. On the other hand, he doesn't want me to go straight to what he likes. I have to seem to stumble across it.

So I'll open *The Joy of Cooking* at page 422, say, and read out 'Lamb Forestière or Mock Venison'. Just the title, not the recipe. I won't look up for a response, but I'll be aware of him. Then 'Braised Leg of Lamb', then 'Braised Lamb Shanks or Trotters', then 'Lamb Stew or Navarin Printanier'. Nothing – but nothing is what I expect. Then 'Irish Stew', and I'll sense him lift his head slightly. 'Four to Six servings,' I'll respond. 'This famous stew is not browned. Cut into 1½ inch cubes: 1½lbs lamb or mutton.'

'Can't get mutton nowadays,' he'll say.

And for a moment I'll be happy. Only a moment, but that's better than not at all, isn't it?

Then I'll continue. Onions, potatoes, peel and slice, heavy pan, salt and pepper, bay leaf, finely chopped parsley, water or stock.

'Stock,' he'll say.

'Stock,' I'll repeat. Bring to boil. Cover closely. Two and a half hours, shake the pot periodically. All moisture absorbed.

'That's it,' he'll agree. 'All moisture absorbed.' He says it slowly, making it sound like a piece of philosophy.

He was always proper, as I say. Some people pointed the finger when we first met; jokes about doctors and nurses. But it wasn't like that. Besides, eight hours a day walking back and forth to reception, mixing amalgam and holding the saliva drain may be a turn-on to some people but it used to give me a bad back. And I didn't think he was interested. And I didn't think I was interested either.

Pork Tenderloin with Mushrooms and Olives. Pork Chops Baked in Sour Cream. Braised Pork Chops Creole. Braised Devilled Pork Chops. Braised Pork Chops With Fruit.

'With fruit,' he'll repeat, making his face into a funny snarl, pushing out his lower lip. 'Foreign muck!'

He doesn't mean it, of course. Or he didn't mean it. Or

APPETITE

he wouldn't have meant it. Whichever one's correct. I
remember my sister Faith asking me when I first went to
work for him what he was like, and I said, 'Well, I suppose
he's a cosmopolitan gentleman.' And she giggled, and I said,
'I don't mean he's Jewish.' I just meant that he travelled, and
went to conferences, and had new ideas like playing music
or having nice pictures on the wall and that day's newspapers
in the waiting-room instead of yesterday's. He also used to
make notes after the patient had left: not just on the treat-
ment, but on what they'd talked about. So that the next time
they could continue the conversation. Everyone does this
nowadays, but he was one of the first. So when he says
Foreign Muck and makes a face he doesn't really mean it.

He was married already, and we worked together, so
people made assumptions. But it wasn't like you think. He
had terrible guilt about the marriage breaking up. And
contrary to what She always said and the world believed,
we didn't have an affair. I was the impatient one, I don't
mind admitting. I even thought he was a bit repressed. But
he said to me one day, 'Viv, I want to have a long affair with
you. After we're married.' Isn't that romantic? Isn't that the
most romantic thing you've ever heard? And there wasn't
anything wrong with him when push came to shove, in case
you're wondering.

When I first started reading to him, it wasn't like it is
now, with him just repeating a word or two, or making a
comment. I'd only have to hit the right phrase, like egg
croquettes or braised tongue or fish curry or mushrooms à
la grecque, and he'd be off. No knowing how long. And the
things he'd remember. Once, I'd barely got started on Chou-
fleur Toscana ('Prepare the cauliflower in the French way
and blanch for 7 minutes') when he was up and running. He
remembered the colour of the tablecloth, the way the ice-
bucket was clipped to the table, the waiter's lisp, the fritto

163

misto of vegetables, the rose-seller, and the paper cylinders of sugar that came with the coffee. He remembered that the church on the other side of the piazza was being prepared for a fashionable wedding, that the Italian Prime Minister was trying to form his fourth government in a period of sixteen months, and that I'd taken off my shoes and run my toes up his bare calf. He remembered all that, and because he did, I did too, at least for a while. Later it got rubbed out, or I wasn't sure if I trusted it, or believed it any more. That's one of the troubles with this.

No, there wasn't any hanky-panky in the surgery, that's for sure. He was always, as I say, proper. Even after I knew he was interested. And he knew I was interested. He always insisted we keep things separate. In the surgery, in the waiting-room, we were colleagues and we'd only talk about work. Early on, I made a comment, about dinner the previous night or something. Not that there was a patient present, but he just froze me out. Asked me for some x-rays I knew he didn't need. That was how it was, until he'd locked up for the night. Liked to keep things separate, you see.

Of course, all that was a long time ago. He's been retired for ten years now, and we've had separate beds for the last seven. Which was more his choice than mine. He said I kicked out in my sleep, and that when he woke up he liked to listen to the World Service. I suppose I didn't mind too much, because by this time we were only companionable, if you know what I mean.

So you can imagine the surprise, one night, when I was tucking him up – this was shortly after I started reading to him – and he said, just like that, 'Come in with me.'

'You're a sweetie,' I said, but not taking any notice.

'Come in with me,' he repeated. 'Please.' And he gave me a look – one of those looks from years before.

'I'm not . . . ready,' I said. I didn't mean it like in the old days, I meant that I wasn't prepared, in other ways. All sorts of ways. Who would be, after such a time?

'Go on, turn out the light and take your clothes off.'

Well, you can imagine what I thought. I assumed it must be something to do with the drugs. But then I wondered, maybe not, maybe it's because of what I've been reading to him, and the way the past's been coming back, and perhaps this moment, this hour, this day is for him suddenly like it was back then. And the idea that it might be just melted me. I wasn't in any right sort of state – I wasn't wanting him – it doesn't work like that, but I couldn't not. So I turned out the light and stood there in the dark taking off my clothes, and I could hear him listening if you know what I mean. And *that* was sort of exciting, this listening silence, and finally I took a breath and untucked the covers and got in beside him.

He said, and I'll remember it until my dying day, he said, in that dry voice of his, as if I'd started talking private life in the surgery, he said, 'No, not you.'

I thought I'd misheard, and then he said again, 'No, not you, you bitch.'

That was a year or two ago, and there's been worse, but that was the worst, if you know what I mean. I just got out of bed and ran to my room, leaving my clothes in a pile next to his bed. He could work that out for himself in the morning, if he cared to. Not that he did, or remembered. Shame doesn't come into it, not any more.

'Cole Slaw,' I read. 'Oriental Bean Sprout Salad. Chicory and Beetroot Salad. Wilted Greens. Western Salad. Caesar Salad.' He lifts his head a little. I go on. 'Four servings. For this famous recipe from California, leave: 1 clove garlic, peeled and sliced, in ¾ cup olive oil: none other.'

'Cup,' he repeats. By which he means he doesn't like the way Americans give measures in cups, any fool knows how the size of a cup can vary. He's always been like that, very precise. If he was cooking and a recipe said. 'Take two or three spoonfuls of something', he'd get ratty because he'd want to know if two was right or three was right, they can't both be right, can they, Viv, one must be better than the other, it's logical.

Sautée the bread. Two heads of romaine, salt, dry mustard, generous gratings of pepper.

'Generous,' he repeats, meaning as above.

Five fillets of anchovy, three tablespoons wine vinegar.

'Less.'

One egg, two to three tablespoons parmesan cheese.

'Two *to* three?'

'The juice of a lemon.'

'I like your figure,' he says. 'I've always been a tit man.'

I don't take any notice.

The first time I did him Caesar Salad, it worked wonders. 'You flew Pan Am., I'd been at an Oral B conference in Michigan, and you joined me, and we were driving from nowhere to nowhere, deliberately.' That was one of his jokes. You see, he'd always want to know what we were doing, and when, and why, and where. Nowadays they'd call him a control freak, but most people were like that then. Once I said to him, why can't we be more spontaneous, just take off for a change? And he'd given his little smile and said, 'Very well, Viv, if that's what you want, we'll go from nowhere to nowhere, deliberately.'

He remembered Dino's Diner, just off the interstate, way down South. We'd stopped for lunch. He remembered our waiter, Emilio, who said he'd been taught to make a Caesar Salad by a man who'd been taught by the man who first invented it. Then he described Emilio making it in front of us, pounding the anchovies with the back of a spoon, dropping the egg from a great height, playing the parmesan grater like a musical instrument. The last-minute scatter of croutons. He remembered it all, and I remembered it with him. He even remembered what the check came to.

When he's in this mood, he can make things more vivid than a photograph, more vivid than a normal memory. It's almost like storytelling, the way he invents it, sitting across from me in his pyjamas and dressing-gown. He invents it, but I know it's true, because I now remember it. The tin sign, the oil-derrick dipping its head to drink, the buzzard in the sky, the scarf with which I tied back my hair, the rainstorm, and the rainbow after the rainstorm.

He always liked his food. He used to ask his patients about their eating habits, and make a little note afterwards. Then one Christmas, just for fun, he worked out whether patients who liked their food took more care with their teeth than those who didn't. He made a chart of it all. Wouldn't tell me what he was up to until he'd finished. And the answer, he said, was that there was no statistically significant connection between enjoying your food and looking after your teeth. Which was disappointing in a way, because you want connections to be there, don't you?

No, he's always liked his food. That's why *Bon Viveur's London* 1954 seemed like such a good idea at the time. It was among some old books he'd kept, from when he was first setting up in practice, first learning to enjoy himself, before he was married to Her. I found it in the spare room and thought it might bring back memories. The pages smelled old, and contained sentences like this: 'The Empress Club is Tommy Gale and Tommy is the Empress Club.' And this: 'If you have never used a vanilla pod, in lieu of a teaspoon, when stirring your coffee, you have missed one of the million and one small pleasures of the table.' You see why I thought it might take him back.

He'd marked some of the pages, so I guessed he must

have been to the Chelsea Pensioner and the Antelope Tavern and somewhere called Bellometti in Leicester Square, which was run by a fellow known as 'Farmer' Bellometti. The entry for this place begins: '"Farmer" Bellometti is so elegant that he must embarrass his livestock and shame disorderly furrows.' Sounds like it was written a lifetime ago, doesn't it? I tried out a few names and places on him. Le Belle Meunière, Brief Encounter, Hungaria Taverna, Monseigneur Grill, Ox on the Roof, Vaglio's Maison Suisse.

He said, 'Suck my cock.'

I said, 'I *beg* your pardon.'

He put on a horrid accent and said, 'You know how to suck cock, don't you? You just open your mouth like your cunt – and suck.' Then he looked at me as if to say, Now you know where you are, now you know who you're dealing with.

I put it down to a bad day, or the drugs. And I didn't think it had anything to do with me, either. So the next afternoon I tried again.

'Did you ever go to somewhere called Peter's?'

'Knightsbridge,' he replied. 'I'd just done a tricky crown repair on a theatrical lady. American, she was. Said I'd saved her life. Asked if I liked food. Gave me a fiver and told me to take my best girl to Peter's. Very kindly rang up beforehand and told them to expect me. I'd never been anywhere so fancy. There was a Dutch pianist called Eddie. I had the mixed grill Peter's: steak, frankfurter, slice of liver, fried egg, grilled tomato and two slices of grilled ham. Remember it to this day. Fat as a tick I was afterwards.'

I wanted to ask who his best girl had been at the time, but instead I said, 'What did you have for dessert?'

He frowned, as if consulting a distant menu. 'Fill your cunt up with honey and let me lick it out, that's what I call dessert.'

As I say, I didn't take it personally. I thought it might

have something to do with whichever girl he'd taken to Peter's all those years ago. Later, in bed, I checked the entry for the restaurant. He'd remembered it absolutely right. And there *was* a Dutch pianist called Eddie. He played every night of the week from Monday to Saturday. The reason he didn't play on Sunday, I read, was 'not due to disinclination on Eddie's part, or grouchiness on Mr Steinler's, but to the primness of our nationals which stultifies gaiety like an ingrowing toenail.' Is that what we do? Do we stultify gaiety? Mr Steinler, I suppose, must have been the proprietor.

He used to say to me, when we first met, 'Life is just a premature reaction to death.' I told him not to be morbid, we had the best years ahead of us.

I don't want to give the impression that food is the only thing he's ever been interested in. He used to follow the news, and always had his opinions. His convictions. He liked horse-racing, though he was never a betting man: twice a year, the Derby and the National, that was enough for him, couldn't even get him to have a flutter on the Oaks or the St Leger. Very controlled, you see; careful. And he'd read biographies, especially of people in show business, and we travelled, and he liked dancing. But all that's gone now, you see. And he doesn't like food any more; not to eat, anyway. I make him purees in the blender. I won't buy the tinned stuff. He can't have alcohol, of course, that would over-excite him. He likes cocoa, and warm milk. Not too hot, it mustn't boil, just warmed to body temperature.

When it all began, I thought, well it's better than some things he could have got. Worse than others, better than some. And though he'll forget things, he'll always be himself, there, underneath, through and through. It may be like a second childhood, but it'll be *his* childhood, won't it? That's what I thought. Even if it gets bad and he doesn't recognize me, I'll recognize him, always, and that will be enough.

When I thought he was having trouble with people, with remembering them, I got down the photo album. I stopped keeping it a few years ago. Didn't like what came back from the chemist's, if you want to know the truth. He started at the final page, I don't know why, but it seemed like a good idea, going backwards through your life rather than forwards. Back, together, with me at his side. The last photos I'd stuck in were from the cruise, and they weren't very successful. Or rather, they weren't very flattering. A table of red-faced pensioners in paper hats with staring eyes all pink from the flash. But he examined every picture with what I thought was recognition, then slowly worked his way back through the book: retirement, silver wedding, trip to Canada, weekend breaks in the Cotswolds, Skipper just before we had him put down, the flat after and then before redecoration, Skipper when he first arrived, and so on, back and back, until he got to the holiday we took after we'd been married a year, in Spain, on the beach, with me in a costume I'd worried about in the shop until I realized we'd hardly be likely to run into any of his colleagues. When I'd first put it on I couldn't believe what it showed. Still, I decided to go for it, and . . . well, let's just say that I didn't have any complaints about its effect on marital relations.

Now, he stopped at the photo, peered at it for a long time, then looked up at me. 'I could really do *her* tits,' he said.

I'm not a prude, whatever you might think. What shocked me wasn't the 'tits'. And after I'd got over it, it wasn't the 'her' either. It was the 'do'. That was what shocked me.

He's good with other people. I mean, he's proper with them. Gives them a half-smile, and nods, like some old teacher recognizing a former pupil but not quite being able to place the name or which year they were in the sixth form. He'll look up at them, and pee quietly into his pads, and say, 'You're a very nice man, he's a very nice man, you're a very nice man,' in response to whatever they say, and they'll go away thinking, Yes I'm almost sure he remembered me, he's still there underneath it all, terribly sad of course, sad for him and sad for her, but I expect he was glad of the visit, and that's my duty done. I'll close the door behind them and when I get back he'll be pushing the tea things on to the floor, smashing another cup. I'll say, 'No, let's not do that, let's leave them on the tray,' and he'll say, 'I'm going to stuff my prick up your big fat arse and fuck you up the bum in out in out and then squirt squirt squirt it up you.' Then he'll give a cackle, as if he'd got away with it just now over tea, as if he'd tricked me. As if he'd always tricked me, all down the years.

From the start he had the better memory, that's the joke of it. I used to think that I'd be able to rely on him, on him remembering; in the future, I mean. Now I look at the pictures of some weekend break in the Cotswolds twenty years ago and think, where did we stay, what's that church or abbey, why did I photograph this forsythia hedge, who did the driving, and did we have marital relations? No, I don't ask the last bit, though I might as well.

He says, 'Suck my balls, go on, take them into your mouth one at a time and diddle-diddle them with your tongue.' He doesn't make it sound fond. He says, 'Squirt baby lotion all over your tits and push them together with your hands and let me fuck you between them and come on your neck.' He says, 'Let me shit in your mouth, you've always wanted me to do that, haven't you, you tight bitch, just fucking let me do it for a change.' He says, 'I'll pay you to do what I want, but you can't pick and choose, you have to do everything, I'll pay you, I've got my lump-sum pension, no point leaving it for *her*.' By 'her' he doesn't mean Her. He means me.

I'm not worried about that. I've got power of attorney. Except that when he gets worse I'll have to pay for nursing. And depending how long he lives, I may well spend it all. No point leaving any for *her* indeed. I expect I'll find myself doing sums. Like: twenty or thirty years ago he spent two or three days working with all the skill and concentration at his disposal to earn money I'll now spend in an hour or two getting a nurse to wipe his bottom and put up with the jabber of a naughty five-year-old. No, that's not right. A naughty seventy-five-year-old.

He said, all that time ago, 'Viv, I want to have a long affair with you. After we're married.' On our wedding night he unwrapped me like a present. He was always tender. I used to smile at his ways, I'd say, 'It's all right, I don't need an anaesthetic for this.' But he didn't like me making jokes in bed, so I stopped. I think in the end he took it more seriously than I did. I mean, there's nothing wrong with me in that department either. I just think you should be allowed to laugh if the need arises.

What's happened now, if you want to know the truth, is that I'm finding it hard to remember what we were like in bed together. It seems like something other people did. People wearing clothes they thought fashionable but which now seem silly. People who went to Peter's and heard Eddie the Dutch pianist play every night except Sunday. People who stirred their coffee with vanilla pods. That strange, that far away.

Of course, he still has his good days as well as his bad ones. We go from nowhere to nowhere, deliberately. On his good days, he won't get over-excited, and he'll enjoy his warm milk, and I'll read to him. And then, for a while, things will be how they used to be. Not how they used to be before, but how they used to be just a while ago.

I never say his name to get his attention, because he

thinks I'm referring to someone else, and that panics him. Instead, I'll say, 'Beef Goulash.' He won't look up, but I'll know he's heard. 'Lamb or Pork Goulash,' I'll continue. 'Veal and Pork Goulash. Belgian Beef Stew or Carbonnade Flamande.'

'Foreign muck,' he'll mutter with a quarter of a smile.

'Oxtail Stew,' I'll go on, and he'll raise his head slightly, though I know it isn't quite time. I've learnt what he likes; I've learnt the timing. 'Beef Rolls, Roulades or Paupiettes. Steak and Kidney Pie.'

And he'll lift his eyes to me expectantly.

'Four servings. Preheat oven to 350°. Classic recipes for this dish often call for beef kidneys.' He'll shake his head in mild disagreement. 'If they are used, they must be blanched. Cut into small, half-inch-thick slices: 1½lbs round or other beef steak.'

'*Or other*,' he repeats disapprovingly.

'Three-quarters of a pound veal or lamb kidneys.'

'*Or.*'

'Three tablespoons butter or beef fat.'

'*Or*,' he says louder.

'Seasoned flour. Two cups brown stock.'

'*Cups.*'

'One cup dry red wine or beer.'

'*Cup*,' he repeats. '*Or*,' he repeats. Then he smiles.

And for a moment I'll be happy.

# THE FRUIT CAGE

When I was thirteen, I discovered a tube of contraceptive jelly in the bathroom cabinet. Despite a generalized suspicion that anything concealed from me was probably related to lust, I failed to recognize the purpose of this battered tube. Some ointment for eczema, hair loss, middle-age spread. Then the small print, flaked of a few letters, told me what I didn't want to know. My parents still did it. Worse, when they did it, there was a chance that my mum might get pregnant. This was, well, inconceivable. I was thirteen, my sister seventeen. Perhaps the tube was very, very old. I squeezed it tentatively and was downcast when it softly yielded to my thumb. I touched the cap, which appeared to unscrew with lubricious speed. My other hand must have squeezed again, as guck squirted into my palm. Fancy my mother doing that to herself, whatever 'that' might involve, since in all likelihood this did not comprise the full kit. I sniffed the petrolly gel. Somewhere between a doctor's surgery and a garage, I thought. Revolting.

This happened more than thirty years ago. I had forgotten it until today.

I have known my parents all my life. That must seem a statement of the obvious, I realize. Let me explain. As a child I felt loved and protected, duly responding with a normal belief in the indissolubility of the parental tie. Adolescence brought the usual boredom and false maturity, but no more than for anyone else. I left home without trauma, and was never out of touch for long. I provided grandchildren, one of each sex, making up for my sister's devotion to her career. Later, I had responsible conversations with my parents – well, with my mother – about the realities of ageing and the practicality of bungalows. I organized a sit-down lunch for their fortieth wedding anniversary, inspected sheltered housing, discussed their wills. Ma even told me what she wanted done with their ashes. I was to take the caskets to a cliff-top on the Isle of Wight where, I deduced, they had first declared love for one another. Those present were to cast their dust into the wind and the seagulls. I already found myself worrying what I was to do with the empty caskets. You couldn't exactly toss them off the cliff after the ashes; nor could you keep them for storing, I don't know, cigars or chocolate biscuits or Christmas decorations. And you certainly couldn't stuff them into some waste-bin at the car park which my mother had also thoughtfully circled on the Ordnance Survey map. She had pressed it on me when my father was out of the room and would occasionally confirm that I was keeping it in a safe place.

Known them, you see. All my life.

My mother is called Dorothy Mary Bishop, and her maiden name was Heathcock, which she gave up with no regret. My father is Stanley George Bishop. She was born in 1921, he in 1920. They grew up in different parts of the West Midlands, met on the Isle of Wight, settled on the outer rural fringes of London, and retired to the Essex–Suffolk border. Their lives were orderly. During the war, my mother worked in the county surveyor's office; my father was in the RAF. No, he wasn't a fighter pilot or anything; his talent was for administration. Afterwards he joined the local authority, eventually becoming deputy chief executive. He liked to say that he was responsible for everything we took for granted. Essential but unappreciated: my father was an ironical man, and this is how he chose to present himself.

Karen was born four years before me. Childhood comes back in smells. Porridge, custard, my father's pipe; washing powder, Brasso, my mother's scent before the Masonic dinner-dance; bacon through the floorboards as I lay in bed; Seville oranges boiling volcanically while there was still frost on the ground outside; drying mud entwined with grass on football boots; bog-pongs from previous users and kitchen-pongs from backfiring waste-pipes; the ageing leather seats of our Morris Minor, and the acrid slack my father shovelled on the fire to bank it up. All these smells recurred, as did the unchanging cycles of school, weather, garden-growth and domesticity. The first scarlet break of runner-bean flowers; folded vests in my bottom drawer; mothballs; the gas-poker. On Mondays the house would throb to our washing machine, which used to crab itself berserkly across the kitchen floor, howling and bucking, before sending, at deranged intervals, gallons of hot grey water along its fat beige tubes to spit and gush into the sink. The manufacturer's name on its metal badge was Thor. The god of thunder sits and growls in the outer reaches of suburbia.

I suppose I should try and give you some idea of my parents' characters.

People used to assume, I think, that my mother had more natural intelligence than my father. He was – is – a large man, fleshy and bellied, with bunched veins corrugating the backs of his hands. He used to say that he had heavy bones. I didn't know the weight of bones could vary. Perhaps it can't; perhaps this was just something he said to amuse us kids, or to perplex us. He could seem ponderous, as his thick fingers paused over a chequebook, as he rewired a plug with the DIY book open in front of him. But children quite like one parent to be slow: the adult world then seems less impossible. My father used to take me up to the Great Wen, as he called it, to buy model aircraft kits (more smells: balsa wood, coloured dope, metal knives). In those days a return ticket on the Undergound was marked with a perforation, drawn but not cut; the outward portion occupied two-thirds of the ticket, the return one-third – a division whose logic I could never see. Anyway, my father would pause as we approached the barrier at Oxford Circus and look down at the tickets in his large palm with a gentle puzzlement. I would peck them nimbly off his hand, tear them down the perforations, drop the return thirds back into his palm, and swaggeringly present the outward stubs to the ticket collector. I was nine or ten at the time, and pleased with my sleight of finger; years on, I wonder if, after all, he was bluffing.

My mother was the organizer. Though my father spent his life making sure that the borough ran smoothly, when he closed the front door he submitted to another's system of control. My mother bought his clothes, arranged their social life, oversaw our schooling, budgeted, made decisions about holidays. To third parties my father used to refer to his wife as 'the Government' or 'higher authority'. He would always do this with a smile. Do you want some manure for the garden, sir, prime quality stuff, well rotted, judge for yourself, just feel a handful? 'I'll go and see what the Government has to say,' my father would reply. When I begged him to take me to an air show, or the cricket, he would say, 'Let's refer this to a higher authority.' My mother could trim the crusts from sandwiches without ever losing any of the filling: a sweet harmony between palm and knife. She could have a tongue on her, which I attributed to the accumulated frustrations of housewifery; but she was also proud of her domestic talents. When she badgered my father and he told her not to nag, she would reply, 'Men only use the word *nag* when it's something they don't want to do.' Most days they gardened. Together they had built a fruit cage: poles with rubber balls at their junctions, an acre of netting, and reinforced defences against birds, squirrels, rabbits and moles. Sunken beer-traps caught the slugs. After tea they played Scrabble; after dinner they did the crossword; then they watched the news. An orderly life.

Six years ago I noticed a large bruise on the side of my father's head, just above the temple, by the hairline. It was yellowing at the edges and still indigo at the centre.

'What have you done to yourself, Dad?' We were standing in the kitchen at the time. My mother had opened a bottle of sherry and was tying a piece of paper towel round the neck so that it wouldn't drip if my father poured it less than immaculately. I used to wonder why she didn't pour it herself and save the paper towel.

'He had a fall, silly old thing.' My mother pulled the knot tight with exactly the right strength, for she, more than anyone, knew that a paper towel will rip if tied too fiercely.

'Are you OK, Dad?'

'Right as rain. Ask the Government.'

Later, when my mother was washing up and the two of us were watching afternoon snooker on the telly, I said, 'How did you do it, Dad?'

'Had a fall,' he answered, not taking his eyes from the screen. 'Ha, knew he'd go in-off, what do these young lads know about the game? All potting with them, isn't it, no safety skills at all.'

After tea, my parents played Scrabble. I said I'd just watch. My mother won, as she usually did. But something about the way my father played, sighing as if fate had dealt him letters that just couldn't live with one another, made me think he wasn't trying.

I suppose I'd better tell you about the village. In truth, it's more of a crossroads, where a hundred or so people live in formal proximity to one another. There's a triangular green bitten into by negligent motorists; a village hall; a deconsecrated church; a concrete bus-shelter; a post-box with an ungenerous mouth. My mother says the village shop is 'good for essentials' which means that people use it to stop it closing down. As for my parents' bungalow, it's spacious and characterless. Timber-framed, concrete-floored, double-glazed: chalet-style, the estate agents term it – in other words, there's a pitched roof enclosing a large storage space for rusting golf-clubs and discarded electric blankets. The only convincing reason my mother ever gave for living here is that three miles away there is a very good freezer centre.

Three miles in the opposite direction is a shabby British Legion club. My father used to drive over there on Wednesday lunchtimes 'to get out of the hair of a higher authority'. A sandwich, a pint of mild-and-bitter, a game of billiards against whoever happened to be there, then back around tea-time with his clothes smelling of cigarette smoke. He kept his Legion uniform – a brown tweed jacket with leather elbows and a pair of buff cavalry twills – on a hanger in the utility room. This Wednesday routine had been approved, even perhaps decided, by my mother. She used to maintain that my father preferred billiards to snooker because there were fewer balls on the table and so he didn't have to think as much.

When I asked my father why he preferred billiards to snooker, he did not reply that billiards was a gentleman's game, or that it was more subtle, or more elegant. He said,

'Billiards doesn't have to end. A game of billiards could last for ever, even if you were losing all the time. I don't like things to end.'

My father rarely spoke like this. Normally he would talk with a sort of smiling complicity. His use of irony prevented him from seeming deferential, but also from seeming entirely serious. Our way of conversing was long-established: companionable, chummy, oblique; warm, yet essentially distant. English, oh yes it's English, by Christ it's English. In my family we don't do hugging and back-slapping, we don't do sentimentality. Rites of passage: we get our certificates for those by mail order.

I probably sound as if I'm favouring my father. I don't want to make my mother seem sharp, or humourless. Well, she can be sharp, it's true. And humourless, for that matter. There's a nervous trimness about her: even in middle age she never put on weight. And as she likes to repeat, she never did suffer fools gladly. When my parents first moved to the village they met the Royces. Jim Royce was their doctor, one of the old-fashioned sort who drank and smoked and went on saying that pleasure never did anyone any harm until the day he dropped dead of a heart attack while still well short of the average male life expectancy. His first wife had died of cancer, and Jim had remarried within the year. Elsie was an outgoing, bosomy woman a few years his junior, who wore characterful spectacles and, as she said, 'liked a bit of a dance'. My mother referred to her as 'Joyce Royce', and long after it had been established that Elsie's previous life had been spent housekeeping for her parents in Bishop's Stortford, used to maintain that she had been Jim Royce's receptionist and had blackmailed him into marriage.

'You know that isn't the case,' my father would some-times protest.

'I don't know that it isn't. Neither do you. She probably poisoned the first Mrs Royce to get her hooks into him.'

'Well, I think she's a good-hearted woman.' Faced with my mother's eye and silence, he added, 'Maybe a little boring.'

'Boring? Like watching the test card. Except it's going yack yack yack at you all the time. And that hair comes out of a bottle.'

'Does it?' My father was visibly surprised by this allegation.

'Oh, you men. Did you think that colour exists in nature?'

'I never thought about it.' Dad was quiet for a while. Uncharacteristically, my mother kept him company, then finally said, 'And now that you have?'

'Have what?'

'Thought about it. Joyce Royce's hair.'

'Oh. No, I was thinking of something else.'

'And are you going to share the benefit with the rest of the human race?'

'I was wondering how many U's there are in Scrabble.'

'Men,' replied my mother. 'There's only an A and an E, clothead.'

My father smiled at this. You see how they were together?

I asked my father how the car was running. He was seventy-eight at the time, and I wondered how much longer they would let him drive.

'Engine's running well. Bodywork's not too good. Chassis's rusting.'

'And how are you, Dad?' I was trying to avoid the direct question, but somehow failed.

'Engine's running well. Bodywork's not too good. Chassis's rusting.'

Now he lies in bed, sometimes in his own green-striped pyjamas, more often in a poorly fitting pair inherited from someone else – someone dead, perhaps. He winks at me as he always did and calls people 'Dear'. He says, 'My wife, you know. Many happy years.'

My mother would talk practically of the Four Last Things. That's to say, the Four Last Things of modern life: making a will, planning for old age, facing death, and not being able to believe in an afterlife. My father was finally prevailed upon to make a will when he was over sixty. He never referred to death, at least not in my hearing. As for the afterlife: on the rare occasions we entered a church as a family (and only for marriage, baptism or funeral), he would kneel for a few moments with his fingers pressed to his forehead. Was this prayer, some secular equivalent, or just a leftover habit from childhood? Perhaps it showed courtesy, or an open mind? My mother's attitude to the mysteries of the spirit was less ambiguous. 'Poppycock.' 'Load of mumbo-jumbo.' 'Not having any of that done over me, you understand, Chris?' 'Yes, Mum.'

What I ask myself is: behind my father's reticence and winks, behind the jokey kowtowing to my mother, behind the evasions – or, if you prefer, good manners – in the face of the four last things, was there panic and mortal terror? Or is this a stupid question? Is anyone spared mortal terror?

After Jim Royce died, Elsie attempted to keep up with my parents. There were invitations to tea, and sherry, and to view the garden; but my mother always declined.

'We only put up with her because we liked him,' she said.

'Oh, she's pleasant enough,' my father would reply. 'There's no harm in her.'

'There's no harm in a bag of peat. Doesn't mean you have to go round and have a glass of sherry with it. Anyway, she's got what she wants.'

'What's that?'

'His pension. She'll be comfortable now. Doesn't need Muggins here to help pass the time of day.'

'Jim would have liked us to keep in touch.'

'Jim's well out of it. You should have seen the expression on his face when she got yacking. You could hear his mind wandering.'

'I thought they were very fond.'

'So much for your powers of observation.'

My father gave me a wink.

'What are you winking at?'

'Winking? Me? Would I do such a thing?' My father turned his head another ten degrees and winked again.

What I'm trying to get a line on is this: part of my father's behaviour was always to deny his behaviour. Does that make sense?

The discovery was made in the following way. It was a question of bulbs. A friend in a neighbouring village offered to pass on some surplus narcissi. My mother said my father would pick them up on his way back from the British Legion. She rang the club and asked to speak to my father. The secretary said he wasn't there. When someone gives my mother an answer she isn't expecting, she tends to ascribe it to the stupidity of her interlocutor.

'He's playing billiards,' she said.

'No he isn't.'

'Don't be a clothead,' said my mother, and I can imagine her tone all too well. 'He always plays billiards on a Wednesday afternoon.'

'Madam,' is what she heard next. 'I have been secretary

of this club for the past twenty years, and in all that time billiards has never been played on a Wednesday afternoon. Monday, Tuesday, Friday, yes. Wednesday, no. Do I make myself clear?'

My mother was eighty when she had this conversation, and my father eighty-one.

'You come and talk some sense into him. He's going gaga. I'd like to strangle the bitch.' And there I was again. Me again, as before, not my sister. But it wasn't wills, this time, or power of attorney or sheltered housing.

My mother had that high nervous energy that crises bring: a mixture of anxious fizz and underlying exhaustion, each of which fuels the other. 'He won't listen to reason. He won't listen to anything. I'm going to prune the blackcurrants.'

My father moved swiftly out of his chair. We shook hands, as we always do. 'I'm glad you've come,' he said. 'Your mother won't listen to reason.'

'I'm not the voice of reason,' I said. 'So don't expect too much.'

'I don't expect anything. Just glad to see you.' Such a rare expression of direct pleasure from my father alarmed me. So did the way he sat foursquare in his chair; normally he was aslant, or askance, like his eyes and his mind. 'Your mother and I are separating. I'm going to live with Elsie. We'll split the furniture and divide the bank balance. She can live in this place, which I must tell you I've never much liked, for as long as she wants to. Of course half of it's mine, so if she wanted to move she'd have to find somewhere smaller. She could have the car if she knew how to drive, but I doubt that's a viable option.'

'Dad, how long has this been going on?'

He looked at me without a blink or blush and shook his head faintly. 'I'm afraid that's none of your business.'

'Of course it is, Dad. I'm your son.'

'True. Perhaps you're wondering if I'm going to make a new will. I'm not planning to. Not at the moment. All that's happening is I'm going to live with Elsie. I'm not divorcing your mother or anything like that. I'm just going to live with Elsie.' The way he pronounced her name made me realize that my task – or at least, the task my mother had proposed – was not going to succeed. There was no guilty hesitation or false emphasis when he spoke her name; 'Elsie' sounded as solid as flesh.

'What would Mum do without you?'

'Paddle her own canoe.' He didn't say it harshly, just with a crispness implying that he'd worked everything out already and others would agree if only they gave it enough thought. 'She can be a government of one.'

My father had never shocked me, except once: through the window I'd seen him wringing the neck of a blackbird he'd caught in the fruit cage. I could tell he was swearing too. Then he'd tied the bird to the netting by its feet, and let it dangle upside down to discourage other looters.

We talked some more. Or rather, I talked and my father listened as if I were one of those kids who comes to the door with a sports bag full of dusters, chamois leathers and ironing-board covers, purchase of which, their spiel hints, will keep them away from a life of crime. By the end, I knew how they felt when I closed the door in their faces. My father had listened politely while I praised the articles in my bag, but he didn't want to buy. Finally, I said, 'But you will think it over, Dad? Give it a bit of time?'

'If I give it a bit of time I'll be dead.'

There'd always been a kindly distance to our dealings since I became an adult; things were left unsaid, but an amiable equality presided. Now there was a new gulf between us. Or perhaps it was the old one: my father had become a parent again, and was reasserting his greater knowledge of the world.

'Dad, none of my business and all that, but is it . . . physical?'

He looked at me with those clear grey-blue eyes, not reproachfully, just steadily. If one of us was going to blush, it was me. 'It *is* none of your business, Chris. But since you ask, the answer is Yes.'

'And . . . ?' I couldn't go on. My father wasn't some middle-aged friend drooling over totty; he was my eighty-one-year-old progenitor, who after fifty or so years of marriage was leaving home for a woman somewhere in her mid-sixties. I was afraid even to formulate the questions.

'But . . . why now? I mean, if it's been going on all these years . . .'

'All what years?'

'All the years you're supposed to have been down the club playing billiards.'

'I mostly was down the club, son. I said billiards to make things simpler. Sometimes I just sat in the car. Looking at a field. No, Elsie is . . . recent.'

Later, I dried the dishes for my mother. As she handed me a Pyrex casserole lid, she said, 'I expect he's using that stuff.'

'What stuff?'

'You know. That stuff.' I put the lid down and held my hand out for a saucepan. 'It's in the papers. Rhymes with Niagara.'

'Ah.' One of the easier crossword clues.

'They say all over America old men are running around like buck rabbits.' I tried not to think of my father as a buck rabbit. 'All men are fools, Chris, and they only change by getting more foolish with every year that passes. I wish I'd paddled my own canoe.'

Later, in the bathroom, I opened the mirrored door of a corner cupboard and peered in. Haemorrhoid cream, shampoo for delicate hair, cotton wool, a mail-order copper bracelet against arthritis . . . Don't be ridiculous, I thought. Not here, not now, not my father.

At first I thought: he's just another case, just another man tempted away by ego, novelty, sex. The age thing makes it seem different, but it isn't really. It's ordinary, banal, tacky.

Then I thought: what do I know? Why make the assumption that my parents don't – didn't – have sex any more? They still shared the same bed until this happened. What do I know about sex at that age? Which left the question: which is worse for my mother, to give up sex at, let's say, sixty-five, and discover fifteen years later that your husband is off with a woman of the age you were when you gave up; or still to be having sex with your husband after half a century, only to discover he's having a bit on the side?

And after that I thought: what if it isn't really about sex? Would I have been less squeamish if my father had said, 'No, son, it isn't physical at all, it's just that I've fallen in love.' The question I'd asked, and which seemed hard enough at the time, was actually the easier one. Why make the assumption that the heart shuts down alongside the genitals? Because we want – need – to see old age as a time of serenity? I now think this is one of the great conspiracies of youth. Not just of youth, but of middle age too, of every single year until that moment when we admit to being old ourselves. And it's a wider conspiracy because the old collude in our belief. They sit there with a rug over their knees, nodding subserviently and agreeing that their revels now are ended. Their movements have slowed and the blood has thinned. The fires have gone out – or at least a shovelful of slack has been piled on for the long night ahead. Except that my father was declining to play the game.

I didn't tell my parents I was going to see Elsie.

'Yes?' She stood at the reeded-glass door, arms crossed beneath her bosom, head high, absurd spectacles glinting in the sun. Her hair was the colour of autumnal beech and, as I now saw, thinning at the crown. Her cheeks were powdered, but not enough to camouflage the occasional star-burst of capillaries.

'Could we have a talk? I . . . My parents don't know I'm here.'

She turned without a word, and I followed her seamed stockings along a narrow hall to the lounge. Her bungalow was laid out in exactly the same way as my parents': kitchen on the right, two bedrooms straight ahead, utility room next to the bathroom, lounge to the left. Perhaps the same builder had put them both up. Perhaps all bungalows are much the same. I'm no expert.

She sat on a low black leather chair and instantly lit a cigarette. 'I warn you, I'm too old to be lectured.' She was wearing a brown skirt and cream blouse with large display earrings in the shape of snail-shells. I had met her twice before, and been reasonably bored by her. No doubt she was by me too. Now I sat opposite, refused a cigarette, tried to view her as a temptress, home-wrecker, village scandal, but saw instead a woman in her mid-sixties, plump, slightly nervous, more than slightly hostile. Not a temptress – and not a younger version of my mother either.

'I haven't come to lecture you. I suppose I'm trying to understand.'

'What's there to understand? Your father's coming to live with me.' She took an irritated puff at her cigarette, then snatched it from her mouth. 'He'd be here now if he wasn't such a nice man. Said he had to let you all get used to the idea.'

'They've been married a very long time,' I said, in as neutral a tone as I could manage.

'You don't leave what you still want,' said Elsie curtly. She took another quick puff and looked at the cigarette in half-disapproval. Her ashtray was suspended over the chair-arm by a leather strap with weights at each end. I wanted it to be stuffed full of butts louchely smeared with scarlet lipstick. I wanted to see scarlet fingernails and scarlet toenails. But no such luck. On her left ankle she wore a support sock. What did I know about her? That she had looked after her parents, had looked after Jim Royce, and was now proposing – or so I assumed – to look after my father. Her lounge contained a large number of African violets planted in yoghurt pots, an excess of plumped cushions, a couple of stuffed animals, a cocktail-cabinet telly, a pile of gardening magazines, a cluster of family photos, a built-in electric fire. None of it would have been amiss in my parents' house.

'African violets,' I said.

'Thank you.' She seemed to be waiting for me to say something which would give her grounds for attack. I stayed silent, and it made no difference. 'Shouldn't hit him, should she?'

'What?'

'Shouldn't hit him, should she? Not if she wants to keep him.'

'Don't be ridiculous.'

'Frying pan. Side of the head. Six years ago, wasn't it? Jim always had his suspicions. And quite a few times recently. Not where it shows, she's learned that lesson. Whacks him in the back. Senile dementia if you ask me. Ought to be put away.'

'Who told you this?'

'Well, *she* didn't.' Elsie glared at me and lit another cigarette.

'My mother . . .'

'Believe what you want to believe.' She certainly wasn't trying to ingratiate herself. But why should she? It wasn't an audition. As she showed me out, I automatically put out my hand. She shook it briefly, and repeated, 'You don't leave what you still want.'

I said to my mother, 'Mum, have you ever hit Dad?'

She traced my source instantly. 'Is that what the bitch says? You can tell her from me I'll see her in court. She should be . . . covered in tar and feathers, whatever they do.'

I said to my father, 'Dad, it may be a stupid question, but has Mum ever hit you?'

His eyes remained clear and direct. 'I had a fall, son.'

I went to the medical centre and saw a brisk woman in a dirndl skirt who gave off a quiet reek of high principle. She had joined after Dr Royce had retired. Medical records were of course confidential, if abuse was suspected she would be obliged to inform the social services, my father had reported a fall six years ago, nothing before or since to arouse suspicion, what was my evidence?

'Something someone said.'

'You know what villages are like. Or perhaps you don't. What sort of someone?'

'Oh, someone.'

'Do you think your mother is the sort of woman who would abuse your father?'

Abuse, abuse. Why not say beat up, wallop, smack round the head with a heavy frying pan? 'I don't know. How can you tell?' Do you have to see the maker's name embossed back to front on my father's skin?

'Obviously it depends what the patient presents with. Unless a family member reports suspicions. Is that what you are doing?'

No. I am not denouncing my eighty-year-old mother for suspected assault on my eighty-one-year-old father on the say-so of a woman in her mid-sixties who may or may not be sleeping with my father. 'No,' I said.

'I haven't seen a great deal of your parents,' the doctor went on. 'But they are . . .' She paused before finding the correct euphemism. '. . . they are educated people?'

'Yes,' I replied. 'Yes, my father was educated sixty years ago – more – and so was my mother. I'm sure it's standing them in very good stead.' Still angry, I added, 'By the way, do you ever prescribe Viagra?'

She looked at me as if now sure that I was merely a troublemaker. 'You'll have to go to your own doctor for that.'

When I got back to the village, I felt a sudden depression, as if it were I who lived there and had already grown weary of this jumped-up crossroads with its dead church, brutal bus-shelter, chalet-style bungalows and overpriced shop that is good for essentials. I manoeuvred my car on to the strip of asphalt exaggeratedly known as the drive, and could see, at the end of the garden, my father at work in the fruit cage, bending and tying. My mother was waiting for me.

'Joyce Bloody Royce, well they deserve one another. Pair of dimwits. Of course, this poisons the whole of my life.'

'Oh, come off it, Mum.'

'Don't you Come off it to me, young man. Not until you're my age. Then you'll have earned the right. It poisons the whole of my life.' She would allow no contradiction; she too was reasserting herself as a parent.

I poured myself a cup of tea from the pot by the sink.

'It's stewed.'

'I don't care.'

Ponderous silence ensued. Once again, I felt a child seeking approval, or at any rate trying to avoid censure.

'Do you remember the Thor, Mum?' I suddenly found myself saying.

'The what?'

'The Thor. When we were kids. The way it used to travel all over the kitchen floor. Had a mind of its own. And it was always flooding, wasn't it?'

'I thought that was the Hotpoint.'

'No.' I felt oddly desperate about this. 'You had the Hotpoint afterwards. The Thor was the one I remember. Made a lot of rattling and had those thick beige hoses for the water.'

'That tea must be undrinkable,' said my mother. 'And by the way, send me back that map I gave you. No, just chuck it away. Isle of Wight, clothead. Mumbo-jumbo. Understand?'

'Yes, Ma.'

'What I want, if I go before your father, as I expect I shall, is just scatter me. Anywhere. Or get the crem to do it. You're not obliged to collect the ashes, you know.'

'I wish you wouldn't talk like this.'

'He'll see me out. It's a creaking gate that lasts the longest. Then the Receptionist can have his ashes, can't she?'

'Don't talk like that.'

'Put them on her mantelpiece.'

'*Look*, Ma, *if* that happened, I mean if you died before Dad, she wouldn't have the right anyway. It'd be up to me, me and Karen. It wouldn't have anything to do with Elsie.'

My mother stiffened at the name. 'Karen's a dead loss, and I couldn't trust you, son, could I?'

'Ma . . .'

'Sneaking round to her house without telling me. Chip off the old block, you are. Always were your father's son.'

According to Elsie, my mother blighted their life with her constant phone calls. 'Morning, noon and night, especially night. In the end, we just took the plug out.' According to Elsie, my mother was always making my father pop back and do jobs about the house. She used a succession of arguments. 1) The house was half his anyway, so he had a duty to maintain it. 2) He'd left her without enough money to employ a handyman. 3) He presumably didn't expect her to start going up a ladder at her age. 4) If he didn't come at once she'd walk all the way to Elsie's house and fetch him.

According to my mother, my father was back at her door almost as soon as he'd left, offering to fix things, dig the garden, clean the gutters, check the level in the oil tank, anything. According to my mother, my father complained that Elsie treated him like a dog, wouldn't let him go to the British Legion club, had bought him a pair of slippers he particularly disliked, and wanted him to break off all contact with his children. According to my mother, my father begged her constantly to take him back, to which she would reply, 'You've made your bed and you can learn to lie in it', though in fact she only intended to make him stick it out a little longer. According to my mother, my father didn't like the slapdash way Elsie ironed his shirts, or the fact that all his clothes now smelt of cigarette smoke.

According to Elsie, my mother made so much fuss about the back door swelling, so that now the bolt only went half way in and a burglar could be through that in a jiffy and rape and murder her as she lay in her bed, that my father reluctantly agreed to go over. According to Elsie, my father swore that this was the last time ever, and that as far as he was concerned the whole bloody house could burn to the ground, preferably with my mother inside it, before he would be persuaded to drive over again. According to Elsie, it was while my father was working on the back door that my mother hit him over the head with an unknown instrument, then left him lying there, hoping he would die, and only called the ambulance several hours later.

According to my mother, my father kept pestering her to get the back door fixed and said he didn't like to think of her there alone at nights and the whole matter would be resolved if only she'd let him come back. According to my mother, my father turned up unexpectedly one afternoon with his toolbox. They sat and talked for a couple of hours, about old times, about the children, and even got out some photos which made them both damp-eyed. She told him she'd think about having him back but not until he'd fixed the door if that was what he'd come to do. He went off with his toolbox, she cleared away the tea things, then sat looking at some more photographs. After a while, she realized she hadn't heard any banging from the utility room. My father was on his side, making a gurgling noise; he must have had another fall and struck his head on the floor which of course is concrete out there. She called the ambulance – God, they were slow coming – and put a cushion under his head, look, this cushion, you can still see the blood on it.

According to the police, Mrs Elsie Royce made a complaint to them that Mrs Dorothy Mary Bishop had assaulted Mr Stanley George Bishop with intent to murder. They had investigated the matter fully, and decided not to proceed. According to the police, Mrs Bishop made a complaint to them that Mrs Royce was going about the local villages denouncing her as a murderer. They had to have a quiet word with Mrs Royce. Domestics are always a problem, especially what you might call extended domestics like this one.

My father has now been in hospital for two months. He recovered consciousness after three days, but since then has made little progress. When he was first admitted, the doctor said to me, 'I'm afraid it doesn't take a lot at their age.' Now, a different doctor has tactfully explained that 'It would be a mistake to expect too much.' My father is paralysed down his left side, has severe memory loss and speech impairment, is unable to feed himself and remains largely incontinent. The left side of his face is twisted like the bark of a tree, but his eyes come out at you as clear and grey-blue as they ever did, and his white hair is always clean and well brushed. I cannot tell how much he understands of what I say. There is one phrase he enunciates well, but otherwise he speaks little. His vowels are contorted, wrung from his slanted mouth, and his eyes express shame at his maimed articulacy. Mostly, he prefers silence.

On Monday, Wednesday, Friday and Sunday, asserting her marital right to the fourth day out of seven, my mother visits him. She brings him grapes and the newspaper from the day before, and when he dribbles from the left corner of his mouth, she pulls a tissue from the box at his bedside and dabs away the spittle. If there is a note from Elsie on the table she tears it up while he pretends not to notice. She talks to him of their past time together, of their children and their shared memories. When she leaves, he follows her with his eyes and says, very clearly, to anyone who will listen, 'My wife, you know. Many happy years.'

On Tuesday, Thursday and Saturday, Elsie visits my father. She brings him flowers and home-made fudge, and when he dribbles she takes from her pocket a white lace-trimmed handkerchief with the initial E in red stitching. She wipes his face with obvious tenderness. She has taken to wearing, on the third finger of her right hand, a ring similar to the one she still wears for Jim Royce on her left hand.

She talks to my father about the future, about how he is going to get better, and the life they will then have together. When she leaves, he follows her with his eyes and says, very clearly, to anyone who will listen, 'My wife, you know. Many happy years.'

# THE SILENCE

One feeling at least grows stronger in me with each year that passes – a longing to see the cranes. At this time of the year I stand on the hill and watch the sky. Today they did not come. There were only wild geese. Geese would be beautiful if cranes did not exist.

A young man from a newspaper helped me pass the time. We talked of Homer, we talked of jazz. He was unaware that my music had been used in *The Jazz Singer*. At times, the ignorance of the young excites me. Such ignorance is a kind of silence.

Slyly, after two hours, he asked about new compositions. I smiled. He asked about the Eighth symphony. I compared music to the wings of a butterfly. He said that critics had complained that I was 'written out'. I smiled. He said that some – not himself, of course – had accused me of shirking my duties while in receipt of a government pension. He asked when exactly would my new symphony be finished? I smiled no more. 'It is you who are keeping me from finishing it,' I replied, and rang the bell to have him shown out.

I wanted to tell him that when I was a young composer I had once scored a piece for two clarinets and two bassoons. This represented an act of considerable optimism on my part, since at the time there were only two bassoonists in the country, and one of them was consumptive.

The young are on the way up. My natural enemies! You want to be a father figure to them and they don't give a damn. Perhaps with reason.

Naturally the artist is misunderstood. That is normal, and after a while becomes familiar. I merely repeat, and insist: misunderstand me correctly.

A letter from K. in Paris. He is worried about tempo markings. He must have my confirmation. He must have a metronome marking for the Allegro. He wants to know if *doppo piu lento* at letter K in the second movement applies only for three bars. I reply, Maestro K., I do not wish to oppose your intentions. In the end – forgive me if I sound confident – one may express the truth in more than one way.

I remember my talk with N. about Beethoven. N. was of the opinion that when the wheels of time have made a further turn, the best symphonies of Mozart will still be there, whereas those of Beethoven will have fallen by the wayside. This is typical of the differences between us. I do not have the same feelings for N. as I have for Busoni and Stenhammar.

It is reported that Mr Stravinsky considers my craftsmanship to be poor. I take this to be the greatest compliment I have received in the whole of my long life! Mr Stravinsky is one of those composers who swings back and forth between Bach and the latest modern fashions. But technique in music is not learned at school with blackboards and easels. In that respect Mr I. S. is at the top of the class. But when one compares my symphonies with his stillborn affectations . . .

A French critic, seeking to loathe my Third symphony, quoted Gounod: 'Only God composes in C major.' Precisely.

Mahler and I once discussed composition. For him, the symphony must be like the world and contain everything. I replied that the essence of a symphony is form; it is the severity of style and the profound logic that creates the inner connection between motifs.

When music is literature, it is bad literature. Music begins where words cease. What happens when music ceases? Silence. All the other arts aspire to the condition of music. What does music aspire to? Silence. In that case, I have succeeded. I am now as famous for my long silence as I have been for my music.

Of course, I could still compose trifles. A birthday inter-mezzo for the new wife of cousin S., whose pedalling is not as secure as she imagines. I could answer the call of the state, the petitions of a dozen villages with a flag to hang out. But that would be pretence. My journey is nearly complete. Even my enemies, who loathe my music, admit that it has logic to it. The logic of music leads eventually to silence.

A. has the strength of character which is lacking in me. She is not a general's daughter for nothing. Others see me as a famous man with a wife and five daughters, a cock of the walk. They say that A. has sacrificed herself on the altar of my life. Yet I have sacrificed my life on the altar of my art. I am a very good composer, but as a human being – hmm, that's another matter. Yet I have loved her, and we have shared some happiness. When I met her she was for me Josephsson's mermaid, cushioning her knight among the violets. Only, things get harder. The demons manifest them-selves. My sister in the mental hospital. Alcohol. Neurosis. Melancholy.

Cheer up! Death is round the corner.

Otto Andersson has worked out my family tree so thoroughly that it makes me ill.

Some consider me a tyrant because my five daughters have always been forbidden to sing or play music in the house. No cheerful screeches from an incompetent violin, no anxious flute running out of breath. What – no music in the great composer's own home! But A. understands. She understands that music must come from silence. Come from it and return to it.

A. herself also operates with silence. There is – God knows – much to rebuke me for. I have never claimed to be the sort of husband who is praised in churches. After Gothenburg she wrote me a letter which I shall carry on me until rigor mortis sets in. But on normal days she offers no rebuke. And unlike everyone else she never asks when my Eighth will be ready. She merely acts around me. At nights I compose. No, at nights I sit at my desk with a bottle of whisky and try to work. Later, I wake, my head upon the score and my hand clasped round empty air. A. has removed the whisky while I sleep. We do not speak of this.

Alcohol, which I once gave up, is now my most faithful companion. And the most understanding!

I go out by myself to dine alone and reflect upon mortality. Or I go to the Kämp, the Societetshuset, the König to discuss the subject with others. The strange business of *Man lebt nur einmal*. I join the lemon table at the Kämp. Here it is permissible – indeed, obligatory – to talk about death. It is most companionable. A. does not approve.

Among the Chinese, the lemon is the symbol of death. That poem by Anna Maria Lengren – 'Buried with a lemon in his hand'. Exactly. A. would try to forbid it on grounds of morbidity. But who is allowed to be morbid, if not a corpse?

I heard the cranes today but did not see them. The clouds were too low. But as I stood on that hill, I heard, coming towards me from above, the full-throated cry they give as they head south for the summer. Invisible, they were even more beautiful, more mysterious. They teach me about sonority all over again. Their music, my music, music. This is what it is. You stand on a hill and from beyond the clouds hear sounds that pierce the heart. Music – even my music – is always heading south, invisibly.

Nowadays, when friends desert me, I can no longer tell whether it is because of my success or because of my failure. Such is old age.

Perhaps I am a difficult man, but not that difficult. All my life, when I have gone missing, they have known where to find me – at the best restaurant serving oysters and champagne.

When I visited the United States, they were surprised that I had never shaved myself in my entire life. They reacted as if I were some kind of aristocrat. But I am not, or even pretending to be. I am merely someone who has chosen never to waste his time by shaving himself. Let others do that for me.

No, that is not true. I am a difficult man, like my father and grandfather. Made worse in my case by being an artist. Also made worse by my most faithful and most understanding companion. There are few days to which I can append the note *sine alc*. It is hard to write music when your hands shake. It is hard also to conduct. In many ways A.'s life with me has become a martyrdom. I acknowledge that.

Gothenburg. I went missing before the concert. I was

not to be found in the usual place. A.'s nerves were shredded. She went to the hall nonetheless, praying for the best. To her surprise, I made my entrance at the appointed time, took my bow, raised my baton. A few bars into the overture, she told me, I broke off, as if it were a rehearsal. The audience was puzzled, the orchestra more so. Then I gave a new up-beat, and went back to the beginning. What followed, she assured me, was chaos. The audience was enthusiastic, the subsequent press respectful. But I believe A. After the concert, standing among friends outside the hall, I took a whisky bottle from my pocket and smashed it on the steps. I have no memory of any of this.

When we returned home, and I was quietly drinking my morning coffee, she gave me a letter. After thirty years of marriage, she wrote to me in my own home. Her words have been with me ever since. She told me I was a useless weakling who took refuge from problems in alcohol; one who imagined drinking would help him create new masterpieces, but was grievously mistaken. In any event, she would not expose herself ever again to the public indignity of watching me conduct in an inebriated condition.

I offered no word of reply, written or spoken. I tried to respond by deed. She was true to her letter, and did not accompany me to Stockholm, nor to Copenhagen, nor to Malmö. I carry her letter with me all the time. I have written our eldest daughter's name on the envelope, so she will know, after my death, what was said.

How dreadful old age is for a composer! Things don't go as quickly as they used to, and self-criticism grows to impossible proportions. Others see only fame, applause, official dinners, a state pension, a devoted family, supporters across the oceans. They note that my shoes and shirts are made for me in Berlin. On my eightieth birthday my face was put on a postage stamp. *Homo diurnalis* respects these trappings of success. But I regard *homo diurnalis* as the lowest form of human life.

I remember the day my friend Toivo Kuula was laid to rest in the cold earth. He was shot in the head by Jäger soldiers and died a few weeks later. At the funeral, I reflected upon the infinite wretchedness of the artist's lot. So much work, talent and courage, and then everything is over. To be misunderstood, and then to be forgotten, such is the artist's fate. My friend Lagerborg champions the views of Freud, according to whom the artist uses art as a means to escape from neurosis. Creativity provides a compensation for the artist's inability to live life to the full. Well, this is merely a development of Wagner's opinion. Wagner contended that if we enjoyed life fully we would have no need of art. To my mind, they have it back to front. Of course I do not deny that the artist has many neurotic aspects. How could I, of all people, deny that? Certainly I am neurotic and frequently unhappy, but that is largely the consequence of being an artist rather than the cause. When we aim so high and fall short so frequently, how can that not induce neurosis? We are not tram conductors who seek only to punch holes in tickets and call out the stops correctly. Besides, my reply to Wagner is simple: how can a fully lived life fail to include one of its noblest pleasures, which is the appreciation of art?

Freud's theories do not encompass the possibility that the symphonist's conflict – which is to divine and then express laws for the movement of notes which will be applicable for all time – is a somewhat greater achievement than to die for king and country. Many can do that, while planting potatoes and punching tickets and other similarly useful things can be done by many more.

Wagner! His gods and heroes have made my flesh crawl for fifty years now.

In Germany, they took me to hear some new music. I said, 'You are manufacturing cocktails of all colours. And here I come with pure cold water.' My music is molten ice. In its movement you may detect its frozen beginnings, in its sonorities you may detect its initial silence.

I was asked which foreign country has shown the greatest sympathy for my work. I replied England. It is the land without chauvinism. On one visit, I was recognized by the immigration officer. I met Mr Vaughan Williams; we talked in French, our only common language apart from music. After one concert, I gave a speech. I said, I have plenty of friends here, and, naturally, I hope, enemies. In Bournemouth a music student paid his respects and mentioned, in all simplicity, that he could not afford to come to London to hear my Fourth. I put my hand in my pocket and said, 'I will give you *ein Pfund Sterling*.'

My orchestration is better than Beethoven's, and my themes are better. But he was born in a wine country, I in a land where soured milk rules the roost. A talent like mine, not to say genius, cannot be nourished on junket.

During the war the architect Nordman sent me a parcel shaped like a violin case. It was indeed a violin case, but inside was a leg of smoked lamb. I composed *Fridolin's Folly* in gratitude and sent it to Nordman. I knew him for a keen *a cappella* singer. I thanked him for *le délicieux violon*. Later, someone sent me a case of lampreys. I responded with a choral piece. I reflected to myself that things had turned inside out. When artists had patrons, they would produce music, and as long as they continued to do so, they would be fed. Now, I am sent food, and respond by producing music. It is a more haphazard system.

Diktonius called my Fourth a 'bark bread symphony', referring to the old days when the poor used to adulterate flour with finely ground bark. The loaves that resulted were not of the finest quality, but starvation was usually kept at bay. Kalisch said that the Fourth expressed a sullen and unpleasant view of life in general.

When I was a young man, I was hurt by criticism. Now, when I am melancholy, I reread unpleasant words written about my work and am immensely cheered up. I tell my colleagues, 'Always remember, there is no city in the world which has erected a statue to a critic.'

The slow movement of the Fourth will be played at my funeral. And I wish to be buried with a lemon clasped in the hand which wrote those notes.

No, A. would take the lemon from my dead hand as she takes the whisky bottle from my living one. But she will not countermand my instruction about the 'bark bread symphony'.

Cheer up! Death is round the corner.

My Eighth, that is all they ask about. When, Maestro, will it be finished? When may we publish it? Perhaps just the opening movement? Will you offer it to K. to conduct? Why has it taken you so long? Why has the goose ceased to lay golden eggs for us?

Gentlemen, there may be a new symphony, or there may not. It has taken me ten, twenty years, nearly thirty. Perhaps it will take more than thirty. Perhaps there will be nothing there even at the end of thirty years. Perhaps it will end in fire. Fire, then silence. That is how everything ends, after all. But misunderstand me correctly, gentlemen. I do not choose silence. Silence chooses me.

A.'s name-day. She wishes me to go mushrooming. The morels are ripening in the woods. Well, that is not my forte. However, by dint of work, and talent and courage, I found a single morel. I picked it, put it to my nose and sniffed, laid it reverently in A.'s little basket. Then I dusted the pine-needles from my cuffs and, having done my duty, went home. Later, we played duets. *Sine alc.*

A great *auto da fe* of manuscripts. I collected them in a laundry basket and in A.'s presence burnt them in the open fire in the dining room. After a while she could stand it no longer and left. I continued the good work. By the end I was calmer and lighter in mood. It was a happy day.

Things don't go as quickly as they used to . . . True. But why should we expect life's final movement to be a *rondo allegro*? How should we best mark it? *Maestoso*? Few are so lucky. *Largo* – still a little too dignified. *Largamente e appassionato*? A final movement might begin like that – my own First did so. But in life it does not lead to an *allegro molto* with the conductor flaying the orchestra to greater speed and noise. No, for its last movement life has a drunkard on the podium, an old man who does not recognize his own music, a fool who cannot tell rehearsal from performance. Mark it *tempo buffo*? No, I have it. Mark it merely *sostenuto*, and let the conductor make the decision. After all, one may express the truth in more than one way.

Today I went for my customary morning walk. I stood on the hill looking north. 'Birds of my youth!' I cried to the sky, 'Birds of my youth!' I waited. The day was heavy with clouds, but for once the cranes were flying beneath them. As they approached, one broke from the flock and flew directly towards me. I raised my arms in acclamation as it made a slow circle around me, trumpeting its cry, then headed back to rejoin its flock for the long journey south. I watched until my eyes blurred, I listened until my ears could hear nothing more, and silence resumed.

I walked slowly back to the house. I stood in the doorway, calling for a lemon.

# JULIAN BARNES

## Talking It Over

PICADOR

*Look, I just don't particularly think it's anyone's business. I really don't. I'm an ordinary, private person. I haven't got anything to say.*

Introducing Stuart, Gillian and Oliver. Each takes their turn to speak straight out to the camera – and give their side of a contemporary love triangle. What begins as a comedy of misunderstanding slowly darkens and deepens into a compelling exploration of the quagmires of the heart.

'Few writers think and talk so beguilingly. This is wonderfully funny. And intelligent. And moving'
***Independent on Sunday***

'Quicksilver clever and allusive'
***The Times***

'Scintillating . . . It's funny, quick on the draw, and knows when to soften its gaze. It reads so smoothly, the pages seem to flip themselves'
***Observer***

'A writer of rare intelligence. He catches the detail of contemporary life with an uncanny forensic skill . . . He is, as always, a superb ironist, a connoisseur of middling, muddling, modern England'
***London Review of Books***

## OTHER PICADOR BOOKS
## AVAILABLE FROM PAN MACMILLAN

All Pan Macmillan titles can be ordered from our website,
www.panmacmillan.com, or from your local bookshop
and are also available by post from:

**Bookpost, PO Box 29, Douglas, Isle of Man IM99 1BQ**
Credit cards accepted. For details:
Telephone: 01624 677237
Fax: 01624 670923
E-mail: bookshop@enterprise.net
www.bookpost.co.uk

*Free postage and packing in the United Kingdom*

Prices shown above were correct at the time of going to press.
Pan Macmillan reserve the right to show new retail prices on covers
which may differ from those previously advertised in the text
or elsewhere.